MW00962343

I dedicate this novel to all my friends

You only live once so live your life free and happy the way

you want and never regret anything.

And to all the wonderful women that have entered my life
through the years

Bridget Mcbride

Melissa Wanzer

Rebecca McDaniels

Sherise schleining

CHAPTER ONE

"Welcome, I am Cassandra" said the 5'8" strawberry blonde, standing at the door.

Cassandra was wearing a white silk slip that was see through, you noticed that both of her nipples on her breast were pierced and connected with a gold chain to each other, then you could make out a couple of diamonds hanging from her piercing on her clit.

"Hello, this is Kelly Copulov, and I am Sasha Copulov, we came here to spice up our sex life. And to fix our relationship "Sasha said in slight American Russian ascent.

She was a medium height brunette, wearing very conservative clothing and her girlfriend was in clothes that you find at a burlesque show in the 19th century that really didn't go with her sandy blonde hair.

Cassandra looking both women up and down, she replies. "Well you two came to the right place, I will need to do some work on both of you first, before any of the techniques can be taught. The first thing to learn in a relationship is that people have to know themselves first, so come on in and we'll get started."

"Thank you" Sasha replied and they walked in passing Cassandra.

Cassandra shut the door, and locked it, she then walked towards Kelly and Sasha taking their hands and she walked in to the middle of them.

"So I have one more question who is it that sent you to me?" Cassandra asked

Both Kelly and Sasha looked at each and gave off a little giggle. Then Sasha replied "You come highly recommended, it was   Paige   Sinclair's   ex   Amanda,   and   Paige   even recommended you to us."

"Very well, then they are both good customers, so how are the two vixens doings?" Cassandra asked.

Sasha moved over next to Kelly and took her by the arm, and `Kelly replied this time. "Well, they are fine as long as they are not in the same room together, which is hard, since Paige is a Detective and Amanda is an ADA for city of Seattle."

Cassandra straightens up and says. "Yes, must be I have had to change their days, so that they would not try to kill one another."

Cassandra continues to walk them to a room she opens a door and walks in followed by Kelly and Sasha. The Room is very large, about the average size of a living room. In the right corner next to the door is table that has many different styles and colours of candles on it. Then there is a full size bed against the far wall that has been stripped bare. There is only one light in the room and that is hanging from the ceiling.

And last there is another table that has nothing on it. Cassandra closes the door behind them.

"okay ladies first thing you two are going to do is to strip, I want you both to take off all of your clothes and place them on that empty table over there., and then I will be back to tell you what to do next." Cassandra opens the door again, then leaves but this time she locks the door after she leaves the room.

Kelly and Sasha hear the door being locked. "Kelly she locked the door." Sasha said sounding a bit scared.

"Yes, but remember what Amanda said, don't panic and do whatever Mistress Cassandra says, So we should start to take our clothes off." Kelly answered.

Sasha nodded, and they both started to remove their clothes. Sasha went first removing her shoes and then her nylons. Then Kelly removed her black leather boots, and her fishnet stockings. Kelly removed her outfit exposing her perking breast.

"Hey look honey, my nipples are perky" Kelly said as she flicked them a little.

"No wonder Kelly it's flipping cold in here. My nipples are pointy too." Sasha added as she took off her blouse showing that she had a baby pink laced satin bra on and her nipple were poking through the lacy area.

Now the two girls were standing next to the table in nothing but there matching light blue silk thong panties.

"Okay now what do we do." Sasha asked.

"I think we are also supposed to remove our panties." Kelly said with a slight giggle.

"What's so funny Kelly; you know how much I hate being naked in strange places."

"Nothing, I just noticed that we have matching panties on, and that we are doing this." Kelly added.

"Yeah, well I love you and I will try anything to work on our relationship." Sasha said as she moved closer to Kelly, placing her hands on Kelly's bare chest, the two women embraced in a long passionate kiss.

"I love you too." Kelly said between the kissing.

They slowly moved over to the bed. "Should we be doing this, who knows Cassandra might want us for something completely different?" Sasha said

"I don't care; we haven't felt this way about each other like this for a long time." Kelly replied.

Kelly laid Sasha gently on to the bed, and continued to kiss her, she moved slowly down Sasha's body stopping at the indent of her neck, gently kissing Sasha's chin too. Then she slowly moved between Sasha's breasts, which she had in her hands teasing her erect nipples.

"Oh god, I love it when you do that" Sasha moaned as she moved and adjusted herself on the bed. Then she added "Please do more?"

Kelly gave off a shy like smile, and then with on swift movement, she started to suck on Sasha's right nipple biting it gently a few times also. Sasha squirmed with each movement of Kelly's mouth on her nipple. Then Kelly moved to the left breast and gave it as much attention as she did to the right one.

"I'm so wet, baby" Sasha let out between the moans.

Kelly continued for a few minutes going back and forth on Sasha's breast, she then slowly move her hand down Sasha's body until she got between her legs and started to rub Sasha's clit and felt how wet she was.

Lifting her head up of off Sasha's breast and replied "You are wet honey."

Sasha swallowed some air before she spoke, then she said "Yes I want you to fuck me now?"

"By all means" Kelly replied and without a second thought and the speed of lightning she had her face between Sasha's Thighs and was tweaking her erect clit with her tongue. Sasha felt shivers go up the sides of her body with each erotic touch.

"Oh fucking god yes, you know what I want."

And for that brief little moment Kelly inserted her tongue inside of Sasha's hole and started to tongue fuck her lover. She moved her hands up and down Sasha's sides grabbing onto the sides of her ass cheeks and giving them a little squeeze. Sasha enjoyed Kelly's feel, it always gave her a wonderful erotic glow, knowing that her lover knew exactly where to touch her. Kelly moved her right hand up towards Sasha's pussy lips started to flick and finger Sasha's clit as she continued to tongue her. Sasha moaned and screamed later, she grabbed on to the sides of the bed each time Kelly made her almost orgasm. Then while Sasha was still in a state of ecstasy, she stopped moved herself back up Sasha's body. They stared into each other's eyes, and then Kelly gave a small smile.

"I want to really fuck, I want to cum at the same time as you?"

Sasha smile back and replied. "I do too baby, I don't know what it is but I want you more then I have ever in a long time."

Sasha sat up, and joined Kelly into positioning themselves in to the scissor form. Their legs were part just far enough apart for their pussy to meet and their clits to touch. They started in rub, moving in as close as possible, the rubbing got faster and faster. Kelly leaned in and hugged Sasha, who in turn did the same thing. Their breast moved and mashed with each others as their rubbing got even quicker. Both women moaned with pleasure, and they shared kisses in between the organisms.

"Oh fuck yes, you bitch fuck me harder?" Sasha screamed in Kelly's ear.

Kelly dug her nails into Sasha's back which made Sasha scream out even more. Sasha's passionately bit Kelly's bottom lip. They continued to fuck each other non-stop for what seemed forever for them.

Kelly moaned out "I'm coming, I'm coming."

"Wait for me" Sasha screamed.

Then without warning, Kelly started to squirt up and all over Sasha's and her bodies. "Fuck, yes me coming."

Then a few seconds later Sasha released her flood gates, and started to squirt her female orgasm juices all over, most of it hit Kelly's breast. Enough went there to where you were able to see some of it drip off the nipples.

"Oh god, don't stop" Sasha moaned trying to catch her breath.

They continued to rub their wet pussies against the other, to where they went through another couple of orgasms, until they collapsed on the bed drenched in sweat and female juices. They held each other tight until they fell asleep. About an hour later as they slept, Cassandra slowly opened the door, and quietly walked in. There was another woman with her, she was 5'9", long read hair that was tied in a pony tail and she was wearing nothing but a pair of Ice pick heeled leather boots. Every time she walked her enlarged clit would rub against her out lips, and would send a pleasurable sensation through her body. Yes she was constantly horny. And she was Cassandra's fuck buddy.

"See Anya, that's all they needed in their relationship, was a way to find each other sexy again." Cassandra said as she moved her right hand over Anya's pussy and started to play with her clit.

"Stop, not here Casey and I guess you're right, I owe you those 500.00 dollars." Anya said in an English Russian mix accent.

"Aye forget it, it wasn't a fair bet, but I will let you make it up in the bedroom." Cassandra said as she continued to tease Anya's clit.

"Okay Cassandra if you don't stop that, I'm going to cum right here." Anya said as she tried to move Cassandra's hand a way.

"Fine we can wait, I have control."

"Yes, but I don't remember I love sex, and can never get enough of it."

Cassandra smiled grabbed Anya's hand and they left the room, closing the door behind them. Cassandra pulled Anya, up a set of stairs and down a long hallway that was lit only with long white candles. Then at the end of the hallway part of the wall slid open and revealed a larger room. This room was very large and white. There was a specially made sex swing that had enough support that it could hold two people in the left corner of the room. A large king size bed was in the centre made up as if royalty was coming to stay. Then a wall of shelves that housed more sex toys then any lesbian could shake a stick.

"Holy shit, Casey I have never seen this room." Anya said in a surprise voice.

"Yes, actually found it a few months ago, and was secretly remodelling it just for us." Cassandra said with a big grin on her face, and then she added. "So do you want to fuck me now?"

Anya looked at Cassandra, moved closer, took Cassandra's hand and placed it between her legs, right where Cassandra had it earlier. "Oh yes god yes, I want to fuck you so bad I can taste it."

"Good because I want you to taste me, in that large bed tonight." Cassandra said as she walked into the room with Anya, closing the door, but not locking it.

Moving very quickly towards the bed, Anya gets on it followed by Cassandra who lies next to her. Anya rolls onto her side, so she is able to look at Cassandra's beautiful naked body, she then takes her left hand and starts trace Cassandra's breast with her fingers tweaking at her already erect nipples. Anya moves a little, putting her mouth on Cassandra's right nipple and started to suck on it, as if it was feeding her. In which it kind of was Cassandra was able to lactate, which pleases Anya who has always liked breast milk. After a minute or two Anya lifts her mouth of the nipple, which is dripping a little bit of milk, and she licks it up with her tongue and then like her mouth.

"Yum, that was good, I love your milk baby." Anya says as she gives Cassandra a kiss adding a little bit of tongue.

"I love it when you suck my milk too, Bunny" Cassandra replied and returned the kiss.

Both of their hands were exploring each other's bodies. Cassandra moved her hands down Anya back, and then rubbed her firm young ass, before she moved between her thighs.

"I so want to be inside you right now, baby I want to taste you cum running down my throat."

"I want you too." Anya said as she opened her legs so Cassandra's hand could get to her clean shaven pussy lips and throbbing clit.

Cassandra obliged Anya with the pleasure of just that, she moves her hand slowly over Anya's pussy, just lightly touching her erect clit. That sent shivers of pleasure through Anya's body.

"Please fuck me I can't stand your teasing."

Cassandra smiled then she moved her mouth just above Anya's pussy, to where she was able to feel Cassandra's warm breathe which turned her on even more. She grabbed Cassandra's head and pushed to her to pussy. Once Cassandra's mouth got a taste of Anya's sweet juices, she knew that it was going to be a wonderful night. Cassandra licked up Anya's juice with her tongue then she gently took her clit between her teeth and pulled making Anya squirm and let out a loud moan. Cassandra then pulled on her clit a little harder, which made Anya move more and even tried to push Cassandra's head down farther then it could go.

"Fuck yes, that's right eat my clit, make me cum in your mouth." Anya shouted

Cassandra continued to bite and lick her girlfriend out, she moved her hands up to Anya's breast, and started teasing and squeezing her hard nipples.

Anya shouts again but this time in Russian "da da ebat', nye as-ta-nof-ka (yes, yes fuck don't stop in Russian)

Cassandra moved a little farther down and inserted her tongue into Anya's hole, licking up the juices there too, and then she began to tongue fuck Anya slowly then quickly. This made Anya grab on to the back of Cassandra's head and pulled her hair. Anya then wrapped her legs around Cassandra's lower back really tight.

"Yes don't stop, make me cum." Anya shouted again as she lifted her lower body off the bed a little, so it would get a fuller impact of Cassandra's face. Then she added "oh fuck yes going to cum."

As Cassandra continued to lick and tongue Anya's hole she could feel the pressure of the orgasm build up and Anya's pussy getting tighter, she knew that Anya was about to cum. And Cassandra also knew that her lover was a real squirter, she would be able to soak, herself and Cassandra all in a short period of time. But then she didn't care, she loved Anya's sweet pussy juices; she loves to try to drink some of it, before

Anya would stop. Then as she gave one more flick of her tongue against Anya's clit she could feel her face getting wet.

"OH, FUCK YEEEES I COMING." Anya screamed as if she was being killed.

Anya squirted just as Cassandra predicted. Her juices soaked the bed, most of her body and most of Cassandra's body. And this time Cassandra was able to hold her mouth over Anya's pussy and catch some in her mouth. Cassandra swallowed Anya's juices and then licked her lips to get the rest of it off. Then she put her face right back down on to Anya's very soaked pussy and began to lick it dry, just loving her lovers juices she was never able to get enough of it. Once she had finished with Anya, she moved her way back up Anya's body. Once she stared at Anya face to face, they shared a few passionate kisses. Then Anya reached over and opened the nightstand next to the bed and pulled out a long silicone strap on.

"Now it's my turn to fuck you and make you cum, my darling." Anya said with a sinister smile on her face.

Anya got up and buckled the strap on on her waist, adjusted the dildo and then she moved Cassandra on to her back, then with no hesitation spreading Cassandra's legs she inserted the dildo into Cassandra's pussy, and began to fuck her. Anya returned the favour for about a half an hour, until Cassandra came, which isn't as messy as Anya coming, see Cassandra doesn't squirt so her orgasms are a bit different but just as intense. Once Anya was finished she removed the strap on, she threw it on the table and got back on top of Cassandra, putting her hands firmly on Cassandra's tits she leaned down and started to kiss her. Cassandra wrapped her arms around Anya and kissed her back. They fell asleep in each other's arms after the passionate sex they had.

The next morning Cassandra and Anya woke to the smell of food. Cassandra got up followed by Anya and they headed to the kitchen where Kelly and Sasha were making breakfast. Sasha turns to see Cassandra and Anya standing in the doorway.

Sasha says in Russian "do-ra-ye-oot-ra (good morning)

Anya returns with the same greeting in Russian also. Then Cassandra looks at her girlfriend then back at Sasha then she replies. "Oh great now I have to listen to Russian from another person."

Anya takes Cassandra's arm and says "Oh come on you love it when I speak Russian, you said the ascent just drives you wild."

Cassandra gives a small smile and adds "yes, but that's you, I didn't expect to hear it in my house from other people."

Anya gives Cassandra a quick kiss on the cheek, and walks into the kitchen. She walks over to Sasha and Kelly. Then she goes and sits down at the long kitchen table. Kelly walks over carrying a couple of plates. She places the plates down. Cassandra finally walks in and sits at the table. Sasha walks over and brings two more plates and a pitcher of orange juice.

Cassandra looks around and then asks "why did you do all of this for?"

"We wanted to, besides it was our way of saying thank you, for what you did for us last night." Sasha replies.

"You don't have to thank me; I did what you ladies needed after not being close to each other for a long time. You two just needed a little nudge. And that is what I do here; give couples a nudge in the right direction."

"Thanks it worked; we haven't felt like that to each other in a long time." Sasha said, with a smile as she looked at Cassandra and then at Kelly.

"You are welcomed Sasha anytime you two need the help I am here and I am cheaper than a marriage counsellor."

"Thank you, so much." Kelly replied.

They all started to eat the breakfast that Sasha and Kelly prepared for them. After the girls finished, Cassandra showed Kelly and Sasha where the shower room was. She handed them a couple towels before Sasha closed the door. Cassandra walked away and back to her room where Anya was just finishing getting dressed. Walking over to Anya and putting her arms around her.

Cassandra asked. "Hey where are you going, we still have the whole day to spend together. Don't leave."

Anya turning around to face Cassandra , who was still holding on to her replied "I have to honey, they need me in court and I have exactly two hours to do what I need."

Cassandra smiled "would that include me"

Anya looked at her and replied in Russian "Bozhe moy, kak ya tebya hochu! no yah nuzh-dah it-ti" (my god, how much I want you, but I must go." Anya then gives Cassandra a kiss on the lips.

"I wish you would speak English when you do that." Cassandra said.

"Why, I know how much my Russian ascent turns you on, I know you don't understand most of it, but I know you love it." Anya finishes the gives Cassandra another kiss and adds as he begins to leave. "Da-svi-dah-ni-ya."

"Bye, now that word I know." Cassandra said to herself, and then added "I so want to marry her."

Cassandra leaves her room and looks for her guest. Looking all over the place, she looks in one last room, which happens to be the private library that came with the house. Sasha is sitting in an old looking chair that looks like it was once in a castle. And Kelly was looking through a very old magick book that was supposed to have been written by Merlin himself.

"Well are enjoying the library ladies" Cassandra asked as she walks up to them.

Kelly looks up from the book and replies "Yes, this library is amazing, so was this book really written by Merlin?"

"That's what I was told when the old owner showed me the library."

Sasha shakes her head "But I thought he was a work of fiction."

Cassandra turns to look at Sasha and then sits in the chair next to her and answers "Most people think he was fake, and that the Arthurian stories were just that."

"But" Kelly interrupted

"But with modern archaeology, they have discovered that there was a real king Arthur and there was a real Merlin, who studied magick and taught. Merlin was a High Druid of the clan that Arthur was a member of. See Arthur was half Roman and half Celt."

"that is fascinating, but how did you get the book".

"when the owner sold me the house and showed me the books in the collection, he said that he wanted to forget about everything he had built here and collected, so I had basically got everything in the house for free for just buying it."

"Wow that's cool" Kelly responded in an exciting voice.

Sasha gets up hands the book she was looking at back to Cassandra and replied "I would like to learn more, but just came here to have help in our sex life. Which you helped, but I have never been a big believer in magick and the supernatural."

That's fine Sasha, I'm not really it's just part of the history of the house. " Cassandra said as she walked over to the shelves and placed the book back on it, then she added. "any time, you girls want to come and use the library, be my guess, consider it a free part of your help."

Kelly grew a big smile on her face and said "Thanks, I just love books."

Kelly closed her book and left it on the table. Then all three girls left the library. Sasha gave Cassandra a hug first then followed by Kelly.

"Thank you for coming, and never let anything get in the way of your girls relationship, I can tell that you two are made for each other. "Cassandra said.

"thank you for seeing us on such a short notice." Sasha added.

Cassandra just smiled then she gave Kelly a hug. "Good bye Kelly, take good care, and I'll see you two later then."

Cassandra walked them to the front door, the door that just a day ago they walked through and entered the house, The day that changed their lives and relationship forever. Kelly and Sasha walked out the door got into their car and drove off. Kelly held Sasha's free hand and they gave each other a smile. By the time they arrived back to their home Kelly had fallen asleep, leaning against Sasha's shoulder. They pulled into the driveway. Sasha turned her head and looked at her sleeping girlfriend, and she said to herself "I don't want to wake her; She is so beautiful when she sleeps."

But then she made up her mind, and gently nudged Kelly awake. It took a couple of times before she would wake up. They Got out of the car, and Sasha helped Kelly up the stair to the door.

"Honey we're home, why don't you go and lay on the couch, and I fix you some tea"

 "And Crumpets" Kelly interrupted.

"Yes and some crumpets" Sasha replied with a sigh to her voice.

Kelly gave that small I'm cute smile to Sasha before she went and laid on the couch in the living room. Sasha heads to the kitchen puts some water on the stove to make the tea, and then she toast a couple of crumpets for her girlfriend.

She says to herself "I don't understand why people like crumpets, but then again I'm sure Kelly doesn't understand why I like Kvass."

The tea pot started to whistle after a few minutes, so Sasha poured the hot water into a tea pitcher and place it on a tray with a couple of mugs, a few tea bags and the crumpets, then she walked out to the living room, where Kelly was sound asleep. So Sasha decided to put the tray back in the kitchen, then she walked back into the living grabbing a blanket off the chair and covering Kelly with it.

"Good night, princess." Sasha said as she leaned over and gave Kelly on her cheek. Then she headed upstairs to their bedroom and added "It was a long day, but at least Cassandra helped us."

Sasha walked over to her desk and opened the middle locked drawer and pulled out a couple of pages. "I guess we won't need these anymore" then she stuck them through the shredder.

"I can't believe you did that" Kelly said standing in the bedroom door way.

Sasha turned around and saw that Kelly was wrapped in the blanket "Oh, I'm sorry I didn't want to wake you"

"No that's fine, but those papers you just shredded them."

"Yes, I don't want a divorce, I want to work out our problems and be the family we wanted."

Kelly walks in to the room farther. "Really you mean that."

"Yes" Sasha says as she walks closer to Kelly and removes the blanket. Then she adds "Come back to our bed, please."

Kelly gave Sasha a big smile, then a kiss straight on the lips. "I love you Sasha."

"I know I love you too."

Both girls embraced in each others' arms gently fall on the bed. They just lay in each other's arms cuddling. They sleep through the night never moving until the next morning; Sasha woke to find that Kelly was not in bed she got up and started down the hall when she heard the shower going and Kelly's beautiful voice singing, as she took a shower.

Sasha opened the door the rest of the way and walked in saying "Good morning princess."

Kelly opened the shower door a little and stuck her head out and replied. "Good morning, want to join me."

Sasha smiled and nodded. She started to remove her clothes and then she got into the shower with Kelly. At first she stayed against the wall not moving, just watching Kelly's gorgeous body all wet and glistening with the soap and water. Kelly turned around and moved closer to Sasha, and with no warning grabbed her and threw her under the shower head.

"Hey what did you do that for?" Sasha said

"I can't be the only one wet and sexy looking, now can I?"

Sasha grinned and then they embraced in a new found passionate kiss. Sasha moved her hand up and down Kelly wet back. Kelly did the same but she took the bar of soap and began to lather up Sasha's body. With each stroke of the soap Kelly flicked Sasha's nipples that were erect by now it was always easy for Kelly to get Sasha in the mood. But before that day at Cassandra's Kelly and Sasha were having marital problems. See it all started one summer weekend when Kelly had met their new neighbour across the street. And this woman was pretty in an average sort of way. Kelly went over there to introduce herself. Kelly knocked on the front door and waited for a few seconds then knocked again. Then the door opened and a tall woman with straight black hair that was tied in a single pony tail answered the door, she was wearing only a black laced bra and a pair of black laced boy shorts.

"Hello how can I help you?" The woman said.

"Hi, I live across the street, my name is Kelly Harrington, I just wanted to say hello and welcome you to the neighbourhood."

"Why, thank you, Mrs. Harrington, my name is April, your last name its Russian right.

"Right, my last name."

"Forgive me but I don't see any Russian features in you."

"Oh, the last name, no my maiden name is Walberg, but I took my partners last name."

"Your `partner!"

"Yes, I am a lesbian; I hope that doesn't bother you, living across the street from a gay couple".

April shakes her head "No, I'm a lesbian too; I had just gotten out of a 5 year relationship with my partner, who left me for violin instructor."

"OH, I am so sorry if there is anything Sasha or I can do, don't hesitate to ask?"

"There is one thing that I could use you help on, if you don't mind."

"No not at all April"

April moves out of the door way and lets Kelly into the house. April checked Kelly out from head to toe. Kelly was wearing a light pink skirt with no stockings on, casual shoes and white blouse that is see through, noticing that Kelly is wearing a purple bra with little pink floral where the nipple would be poking through.

"So if you don't mind if I ask what do you do?" April asked as she walks closer to Kelly.

Kelly replied "right now nothing, I was a school teacher but I left, because we were going to raise a family, then Sasha my partner got a new position in her company and the plans fell through."

April puts her arm around Kelly and gives her a hug as she says "I am so sorry, here come and sit down, and take a load off for a while."

"Thank you"

April walks Kelly to couch and they both sit down. April sits very close to Kelly. She slowly puts her hand on Kelly's bare leg. Kelly turns her head and looks at her; April leans in and gives her a very passionate kiss that Kelly returns. Kelly knows that she shouldn't be doing this but, it feels so good and different.

"I can't" Kelly tried to say

"Can't what, because you're married, so let you feelings go, you know you want to do this." April said as she started to remove Kelly's shirt.

"No, I shouldn't" Kelly insisted but not even trying to stop April.

April slides Kelly's shirt off and cupped her hands around Kelly's breast that were still in her bra. Kelly looked around and then at April, she starts to remove April's bra. She looks down at April's breast and sees that her nipples are pierced.

"Wow did that hurt?" Kelly asked as she touched them

"No, not at all, it did sting at first, but after that they feel great, I don't know what its like not to have them."

"How long have you had them?"

"Lets' See I think I got them when I was a freshman in high school, so about thirteen years."

"Anything else pierced?"

"Well you'll just have to find out!" April says with a smile.

Kelly moves her hands off of April's nipples and placed them on her hips. Then she slowly started to remove Aprils panties, she got them down to her knees. Then there was a knock on the door. Kelly quickly gets up and puts her shirt back on.

April gets up and pulls her panties up. And she goes and answers the door.

Sasha is at the door and she asks "Hello, is Kelly here, she said that she wanted to meet the new neighbour."

April nods and motions for Sasha to come in." Yes she is in the living room we were just talking about the neighbourhood."

Sasha nods "Thank you" she says as she walks in.

Sasha follows April into the living room. Kelly was sitting on the couch when Sasha came in. She immediately stands up and goes over to Sasha.

"Hi honey, we were just talking." Kelly says

"That's what she just told Me." sounding a little angry.

"Please won't you join us" April says

"No thanks."

"Honey, everything okay, you sound angry."

"No, I think we should go now, I need to talk with you."

"Okay, I guess I'll see you later." Kelly said as she looked at April.

Sasha grabbed Kelly by the arm and they walked out of the house, and got to the middle of the street, when Kelly pulled away.

"What the fuck is going on Sasha, you were mean to our new neighbour.

"Mean, I wasn't mean, I wanted you out that house,"

"Then why did you drag me out, we were having a nice conversation."

"Oh I can see, she was walking around in her underwear"

"So, we walk around in ours at home."

Sasha moves closer to Kelly and grabs her arm tight.

"I saw you through the window, she was undressing you and you were touching her tits."

"Well I wouldn't have to if you would touch me more then once in a while, and before you say a word don't even try saying anything in Russian?" Kelly says as she storms up the side walk and into the house.

Sasha looked around and then walked towards the house. Sasha slams the door shut once she gets in side , then she heads to the den where Kelly is on the couch crying.

"What the fuck was that, I catch you trying to make out with our neighbour, and I'm the badgirl." Sasha says as she comes close to Kelly and sits on the edge of the couch.

Kelly looks up and wipes the tears from her eyes. Sasha moves next to Kelly and puts her arm around.

"I am sorry, I didn't realize that I haven't been paying attention to you, but did you did you have to try to make out with that woman."

"I'm sorry to, but she made me feel, like I haven't felt in a long time, I know that letting her make me feel like that was wrong, but we need help Sasha honey , we have been together for eight years and I think we're in a rut. "

The two women give each other a hug, then Sasha says something "if you want we can go a see a marriage counsellor" Sasha said.

Kelly released a small smile and replied. "I would like that, but instead of a regular counsellor, can we go see this woman that Paige said is wonderful at fixing relationships."

"I don't see why not, I don't want to loose you, I love you Kelly"

"Great Paige said her name is Cassandra, and she is very good, she still works with Paige and Amanda."

"Wait, I believe Amanda was telling about this person the other day at lunch, she is good."

Kelly moved closer to Sasha and gave her a big hug "I love you too, honey"

"Kelly promise me one thing, that you won't sleep with our neighbour, or even make out with her any more."

"I promise, I don't wan to lose you either."

Kelly and Sasha exchange kisses. Then Kelly gets up, and heads up the stair.

"Where are you going?" Sasha asked.

"I want to take a nap, before our dinner plans tonight. Want to join me." Kelly replied with a smile.

Sasha got up off the couch and ran up the stairs taking Kelly by the hand, they headed to their bedroom. Once they were in there Sasha closed the door.

Chapter Two

The next morning Sasha and Kelly were in bed fast asleep, Sasha hand her arm draped over Kelly's bare chest. Then the alarm clock went off, and Kelly still asleep moved her hand around until it found the snooze button and pressed it. Then she rolled over hugging Sasha's hand closer to her chest. Moments later the snooze button went off, and this time, Kelly opened her eyes, gently getting out of bed so she wouldn't wake Sasha, she hit the clock off and headed to the bathroom. Ten minutes later Sasha rolled over and woke up after she notice that Kelly wasn't in bed. She gets up and leaves the bed room after putting her robe on , she head to the bathroom, where she can here her lover singing in the shower. Sasha walks into the bathroom.

"Good morning Kelly honey."

Kelly sticks her head out of the side of the door and replies. "Good morning, do you want to join me."

Sasha smiled and nodded; she removed her robe, and entered the shower. Sasha stayed against the wall watching Kelly wash herself. Kelly tuned around as she was just soap up her breast, she stared at Sasha and smiled. Kelly takes Sasha's hand and pulls her under the shower head.

"Hey why did you do that?"

"The reason to take a shower with someone is to actually be in the shower." Kelly said as she moved her hand holding the soap on to Sasha's breast and began to move it around.

Sasha replied moving her hand onto Kelly's hips moving closer. "And to do other stuff."

Kelly and Sasha moved even closer and they began to kiss passionately.

"Do forget honey, we have an appointment with Cassandra tonight, and she said Paige is suppose to be there also" Kelly said between the kissing and the water shooting over their head.

Sasha couldn't stop kissing Kelly, but was able to shout out the word in Russian "Da" (yes)

"That works for me" Kelly finished as she rubbed the bar of soap down the back of Sasha. She started to massage Sasha's back at the same time.

"Kelly dear, we should not now, I have be at work in twenty minutes."

"oh be late it's not like have to be there at any particular time, you're the boss."

"I know"

Then with out warning Kelly moved the bar of soap farther down until it got between Sasha's ass cheeks. Sasha jumped a little then gave Kelly a short smile and continued to kiss her.

"Well I guess I could be late one day."

Sasha slowly helped Kelly to the floor of the tub, and now the water was beating on her back, which kind of felt good.

Sasha moved down to Kelly neck giving her a small hickey she continued down letting Kelly feel some of the water too beat on the top of her chest as Sasha began to suckle on her nipples.

"Oh, yes I love how you do that, you make me so wet."

Sasha looked at thought to her self "that's probably the shower, but I'll take the compliment." She moves her mouth and sucks on the other nipple. Then after a few minutes on the other nipple Sasha moves down Kelly's stomach kissing around her rose and heart belly ring. With out provocation Kelly spreads her legs putting them on the top of the tub.

"I want you inside of me, now" Kelly said in a commanding voice.

This surprised Sasha but with what they have learned from Cassandra in the past two weeks, She has realized that Kelly has taken the role of Dom and she has become the sub, which is fine with her, With out any further command Sasha moved her face to be between Kelly's legs, taking in her lovers sex smell, and savouring every minute of it. Then without any order she moved her tongue across Kelly's erect clit and labia.

"yes that's it slave, lick me good, but I want your tongue inside" Kelly moaned then commanded.

Sasha lifted her head a little and replied "yes mistress." Then she lowered it spreading Kelly's inner lips with her tongue and inserting it into Kelly's hole. Kelly squirmed and released a loud pleasurable moan. Sasha continued to tongue fuck Kelly with out stopping, the water kept pounding onto Sasha's back and hitting Kelly's chest. Then with out warning Kelly pulled Sasha's head off of her and gave a small smile.

"Okay I'm done, you can go to work now."

Sasha gave a Strange look to Kelly as she replied. "What, but I haven't made you cum yet."

"No you haven't but we can do that tonight now you should go before your late."

"You know, your taking this Mistress a little farther than we agreed to?"

"Sorry, I just got carried away. "

Sash got up and helped Kelly up and they gave each other a kiss, then Sasha got out of the shower, grabbed a towel and headed back to their room. Kelly turned the water off , then she got out of the shower, dripping wet. Kelly didn't even bother wrapping herself in a towel, she walked right to the bedroom still wet.   As Kelly walked through threw the doorway Sasha was starting to get dressed. She was putting a pair of ping thong panties on with a matching bra. Kelly walks up to Sasha and touches her pussy with her wet hands.

"I want you to know that I made you wet, while your at work today." Kelly said as she also stuck her hand down Sasha's panties and makes her really wet. Once she is finished Kelly removes her hand and licks Sasha's juices off of her fingers and adds " Well I see that you are already wet again". She then quickly gives Sasha a kiss, and grabs her book from the night stand and leaves the room with out even thinking of getting dressed.

"So I guess I'll pick you up at five tonight, so we won't be late this time to Cassandra's?" Sasha said as she tried to adjust her panties.

"That will be fine" Kelly shouted from the stairs.

Kelly then headed to the back porch so she could sunbath in the nude, like she has been for years now. Sasha finished getting dressed and left the house without saying a word. Kelly looked up from her chair as the door closed , she waited for few minutes and then looked around.

"okay the close is clear!" Kelly said to herself

Kelly put the book down reached over to a small cooler that was sitting next to her chair, she opened it and pulled out a little bag. Inside the bag she pulled out a dolphin vibrator. She turned it on and then moved around her body before she moved down to her clit. Kelly began to massage her clit with her vibrator and then once in a while she inserted inside herself. Kelly did this for almost an hour before she released a powerful orgasm and squirted all over herself and the soaking the chair.

Out of breathe Kelly said to herself "God that was good"

Then she looked around and realized that she hopes that none of the neighbours saw her. Kelly gets up from the chair and looks around a little more, the puts her little toy back into her box and heads into the house. As she walks into the living room, the doorbell rings. Kelly walks to the door and opens it slowly as she hides her naked body behind it.

"hello, April." Kelly says

"Can I come in" April asked.

Kelly opened the door the rest of the way and April walks in looking at Kelly

"did I catch you in a private moment."

"No, besides it's not like you haven't seen me naked, I was just outside reading my book."

"Oh so that's what that noise was , you reading."

Kelly gets a few shades of red. "Um I'm going to go and get a robe on, I'll meet you in the living room?" she says as she begins to head up stairs.

April heads to the living room where she sits down on the love seat. Moments later Kelly comes down in her kimono.

April looks up " I thought you were only going to put a robe on?"

"I did, I still have nothing on underneath" Kelly said as she moved her bare left leg from underneath the Kimono and showed it to April.

"Just tease me why don't you?"

"Sorry can't do that any more , remember we're just friends, no more teasing or flirting." Kelly replied as she undid her obi letting it drop to the floor and then walking over to April so that her kimono would come open.

"So what do you think of my new tattoo" Kelly said as she moved her waist area in front of April.

"Well I like it a black cat with a sword next to your pussy how ironic." April replied.

"Yes, I love it too."

"So what is it suppose to mean Kel?" April asked

Kelly sat next to April letting the kimono slip off and land on the couch. "Well It is suppose to mean that my pussy is always on guard and ready for attacks."

"How cute."

April put her hand onto Kelly's thigh and then she begins to give Kelly a kiss. "I so want you right now, I can't live with your touch, without your skin caressing me."

Kelly slowly moves way, but hesitates and gives in "I want you too, but I really shouldn't I'll be married in a few months, and our sessions with Cassandra are great."

April pulls away "So what are you telling me."

"I'm guess I'm saying I can't and as much as I want this, I think you should go." Kelly said as she began to put her kimono back on. And got up off the couch.

April just looked at Kelly with some sadness in her eyes as she replied " I knew that this day would come, but I was hoping it would be farther in the future."

"I'm sorry but I really do love my fiancé and I don't want any thing to screw up what we have together, I love the time we spend together April but I don't plan on leaving Sasha for you , and I don't think you should have to play this cat and mouse game with me, since our relationship is only sex."

April nodded and started to walk towards Kelly "I agree, but can I give you just one last hug before I go."

"I don't see why not, we can still be friends right."

"Yeah, I would like that very much." Kelly says as she moves towards the door.

April follows and ask "Is it okay if I give you a hug."

"I don't see why not, we're still friends." Kelly responded with open arms.

They gave each other a hug, and April sniffed Kelly's hair a little. Kelly began to pull away, but stopped half way through as they stared at each other, they saw the look in each others eyes and then they kissed once again. April removed Kelly's Kimono and let it fall on the floor. Kelly did not do nothing, she even started undressing April, removing her sun dress, and realizing that was the only thing she had on. Kelly moved her hand up to April's breast and began to caress them, as she use too.

"Yes I like it when you touch my breast, please suck on my nipple." April said

Kelly looked down at April c size breast and without any hesitation obliged her. Kelly began to suck and lightly bite at April's nipples giving then each equal time. April moaned with each touch then she began to lower her mouth and started to kiss Kelly's neck. April grabbed Kelly by the hips and started to move her towards the stairs. They slowly walk up still embraced in each others arms.

"I want you, take me on the stairs. Kelly commanded.

April laid her down as they reached the top of the stairs. Kelly spreading her legs wrapping one around the Stair banner pole and the other braced against the wall, leaving her pussy opened for April. April moves her body down so that her face is staring right at Kelly's wet lips, she took her finger and parted the outer ones and with her tongue started to lick the labia and tease Kelly's clit. Kelly moaned pleasurable, and squirmed about as she was having oral sex done to her. Then without warning a vision of Sasha popped into her head .

"No, No stop." Kelly screamed.

April stopped and looked up, "What's the matter, I thought you wanted me to give you head."

"I do, but I can't I'm sorry" Kelly says as she sits up on the stairs and then adds " I want you so bad, but I can't do this, I have to end it."

"But why, you have been good at keeping it a secret for months, so what's the problem." April ask as she sits on the stairs just below Kelly.

"I love Sasha to much , just right now as you where sucking on my clit, all I could think about is Sasha, and how much I love her."

"I see, I guess it really is over." April says sounding disappointed.

"I think we shouldn't see each other any more either, at least for now, then maybe we can be friends once again."

"Agreed, I think it's for the better." April finished.

April got up from the stairs and gathered what clothes she had removed put them back on and then left the house. She didn't even turn and say anything else to Kelly as she left. Kelly sat on the top of the stairs for a few minutes with out moving and she then started to cry, putting her hands over her eyes trying to cover the tears coming from her eyes. After a few minutes she looked up wiped the tears from her face. Kelly got up and headed to the bed room, she went over to her dresser and opened the drawer, pulling out a pair of light red shear thong panties and a matching bra then she put them on then she went and laid in bed after a few minutes she fell asleep.

Later on Sasha walks through the door, and looks around then she heads up the stairs to the bedroom and saw that Kelly was asleep in the bed wearing what Kelly had always considered Sasha favourite underwear. Sasha looked at how beautiful she looked even when she is asleep. She didn't want to wake her but they did have an appointment to see Cassandra tonight so she had too. Quietly walking over to the bed she leans over and gently gives Kelly a small loving kiss on the lips. Kelly moved a bit, but did not wake up. So Sasha thought of something else, she moved her hand slowly down Kelly's chest lightly touching her breast then she moves her hand farther down placing it onto Kelly's stomach right over her bellybutton piercing. Kelly moved a little more but still didn't wake up. So Sasha did one last thing she could think off, she moved her hand down and inside of Kelly's panties. Place her fingers right on her wet pussy, this time Kelly moved a lot more and then eventually woke up. She looked up and rubbed her eyes and noticed that her girlfriend was feeling her up.

"Hey you finally awake." Sasha said.

Kelly smiled a little and then replied "Yes I was exhausted"

Sasha removed her hand and licked her fingers. "Your still as sweet as you were this morning."

Kelly gave Sasha a big smile, then gets up and gives Sasha a most needed hug and kiss.

"Okay what was all that for, honey?" Sasha asked.

" I missed you today, promise me what ever happens you'll never leave me." Kelly asked has she hugs Sasha even more.

"I promise, are you okay."

"Yes I am now thank you" Kelly finishes as she walks towards the closet and grabs a slip on dress.

Then she adds "Are you ready to meet Cassandra."

"Yeah let me just quickly get changed and then we can go." Sasha replies.

Sasha heads to the bathroom and brushes her teeth and fixed her hair. Then they leave the house and drive away.

April is watching them leave the drive away in their car from her window, then she says to her self "I hope she's happy with Sasha,. Because I will miss her."

A blonde hair woman in Dickies coveralls walks over gives April a tap on the shoulder and says to April. " Well your sinks fixed April."

April turns around and replies "Thanks Jo"

"is there something wrong."

"No it's just that I think my affair has finally broken up with me."

"well that's what you get for sleeping with a married lesbian."

"Thanks Jo you're a lot of help" April said in a sarcastic tone.

"hey what are old friends for." Jo replied in a comical tone.

"I really don't know, but I must do something , I want Kelly back."

April heads past Jo and walks into the kitchen and looks at the sink then turns around and walks back to the living room.

"April what the hell are you doing."

Jo walks over to April grabs her by the arms and gives her a shake. "dear how long have we've known each other."

"Since junior high, I'm guessing what nearly twenty years now." April answers

"Right and how many women have you had since then that were married or engaged to be married."

"are you trying to help or make me look like a slut."

"well I'm trying to help, but if you think you're a slut then "

"I am not a slut, I like women who are married be them gay or straight, remember Allison, she and I had that long relationship until her husband found us together and gave her the choice."

"and she chose her husband and you went into morning and then into stalker mode for a while, until she got a restraining order on you and they had to move out of the state."

"Hey that part wasn't because of me, he had gotten a new job and had to move." April finished.

"Yes dear, but you always seem to get into bad relationships that you truly know will never last, look at you last one, the reason you moved here."

April walks back over to Jo and puts her hand on her shoulder as she replies " and where would a good challenge be if I had a normal relationship."

Jo nods and rolls her shoulders in agreement, then she gives April a short kiss on the cheek before she grabs her tools and leaves.

"I'll see you later tonight, there is a friend of Darlene's that wants to meet you."

"Great another blind date, you know how much I hate them."

Jo walks back over to April and finishes "Yes but it will get your mind off of Kelly, right."

"I guess, Pick me up after your done today then."

"Will do."

Jo leaves April's house and a moment later drives out of her driveway. April looks out her window and then gets an evil smile on her face. She looks around as she walks outside to see if any of her neighbours are looking or even home, once she knows the close is clear April walks over to Kelly and Sasha's house. Walking into the back yard, she pulls the mat up from the backdoor and takes the key that they keep there and lets herself in, disarming the alarm. April thinks to her self that it was lucky that Kelly gave her the alarm code, so if they were ever out, she could check on the house for them. April looks around the house, she then goes up stairs to Sasha and Kelly's bedroom. April opens Kelly's dresser and pulls out a pair of panties, she looks at them and without a second thought sniffs them for a second. Thinking to her self how much she misses that smell already, she looks around a little more she goes and sits on the bed. Looking at the clock she says to herself that she has an hour left before they get home from seeing Cassandra. April unzipped her jeans and lowered them down to her knees then she did the same with her panties, she then took Kelly's panties and started to rub them across her pussy, getting then all wet with her juices. She started to masturbate with the panties inserting then inside of her with each movement and pulling them out. April did this for a few more minutes until she had an orgasm and came on the panties when they were still inside of her, where she left them. April got up and pulled her panties and jeans back up and left the room. Walking through the house, she remembers that Kelly had always talked about being a mother and that she wanted to have a few children with Sasha. Now that is more possible since Kelly broke off her affair with her. April walks around the downstairs for a few minutes and sees the photo of Sasha and Kelly on the holiday celebrating their 5th anniversary of being together. April takes the picture and throws it on the floor, shattering the glass in the frame. Then she walked away.

"Fuck You Kelly." April said to herself as she left the house, putting the key back under the mat, so no one would know that she was there. April snuck back to her house. She went up to her room where she undressed and removed the panties from her vagina. She tasted the sweet juices of her on the panties which made her hot and very horny, so she started to masturbate again this time using the panties as the stimulate. She rubbed her clit and labia hard with the panties. She moaned out loud and even gasped for air a little as she fingered her self with the panties. She stopped for a second and put the panties on. She could feel how wet they really were now.

"Oh god." She said as she started to rub her self above the panties.

April enjoyed doing this for a long time, she even held off to coming a few times so she could have a very large orgasm . Once she couldn't hold it any more she came, squirting through the panties and all over her bed and even herself.

"Fucking aye, that felt good." April said as she laid there out of breathe and energy. She laid there just thinking about her and Kelly in each others arms kissing and making love while

Sasha was out of town or busy with clients of her own. After she got her energy back April got up of the bed leaving Kelly's panties still on and she got dressed again. She then went down stairs into the kitchen and walked over to the fridge and pulled out a container of soy milk. She poured some into a glass, just as she heard her door open. She turns to smile hoping that it was Kelly coming back telling her that she wants her again, but no it was just Jo with a friend of hers. '

"Hey April this is my friend Oksana."

"What kind of name is that?" April asked.

Oksana answered. In a Czech Republic - Russian mix ascent. "It is eastern European Mi' Lady."

April stood there speechless. To her the only Russian speaking woman she has known was Sasha and now she meets this good looking brunette and polite too. April looks Oksana up and down. She is wearing black leather high heeled knee length boots that lace up in the front, Black nylons that are connected to a black laced garter belt. She has on a knee length black satin skirt that flowed with the wind when she walked. And to top it off Oksana was wearing this nice white dress blouse that made the curves of her upper body more visible then most clothes would. Jo gave off a small smile and then Oksana walked over to April and held out her hand.

"I would like to get to know you better, if you let me." Oksana said to April.

April gave off a smile and then replied "I would like that, you look very pretty."

"Thank you, and so do you." Oksana finished.

"good it seems that you two have hit it off, so can we go now." Jo said

"Okay hold your boxer on Jo." April replied.

She looked down at Oksana and saw that her hand was still out, so she took it, and left the house holding hands. They all got into Jo's truck and left. For one brief moment April wasn't thinking of Kelly, but was trying to figure out how to get the hot Russian women to take off all her clothes on the first date. But then again it wouldn't be that hard, she is April, If she can get a straight married woman to sleep with her, then a woman who seems to be interested in her shouldn't be all that hard.

"So is Darlene going to meet us." Oksana asked Jo.

Jo quickly looked over to Oksana and then back to the road and answered. "I believe so, but she said that she might be a little late."

Oksana held Aprils hand a bit tighter, and then she placed her head onto Aprils shoulder. Then she asked "Is it okay to put head on shoulder"

"Not a problem, I kind of like it." April responded.

Oksana smiled and moved her other hand across April's lap. `Moments later they arrive at the party, April nudges Oksana, and they all get out and head to the house. The door opens and a young blonde in barely anything opens the door.

"Hello, and welcome, the host will be with you shortly." The blonde said.

"Thank you" Jo said and so the three of them entered the party. April and Oksana walked in holding hands.

"So I heard that you just broke up with your girlfriend." Oksana said.

April looks at Oksana and then replies. " Yes and I was iffy about this blind date at first, but I'm glad I came."

"I am to, I'm glad to have met you."

Oksana leans in and gives a small kiss then adds. "Kiss okay."

"yes kiss was fine."

They begin to mingle with the others, most of the people at the party are women and a few men. Jo walks over and hugs a few of the women, and gives on a kiss on the lips. Oksana and April move around, April introduces Oksana to more of her friends, and then they spot Darlene so April and Oksana walk over to her and say hi.

"Hey Darlene how's everything." April asked.

Darlene turned and face both of the girls, then she answered. "I'm find and I see that you met my friend Oksana."

"Yes, thank you for having her come, I'm getting to like her." April says as she holds onto Oksana's hand a bit tighter.

"Yes making good friends with her." Oksana replied.

"Good I want you two to have a good time together, and no worrying about Kelly, Okay."

"Yes Darlene don't worry I have Oksana here to keep me busy." April said as she took a glass of champagne off the passing tray, and then she handed one to Oksana, who took and smiled thank you.

"well I'll leave you two alone, and meet others, I need to talk with Rebecca." Darlene said as she gave April a hug and then gave Okasana one too.   Okasana takes April's hand once again and they start walking around talking to people. Okasana whispers something in April's ear and then she walks outside to the large deck that the condo has. Moments later she is joined by April.

"Hey are you okay?" April asked as she walks up to Oksana

"yes things fine, I just wanted to come outside for a little while."

"Mind if I join you."

"No I want you to join me." Oksana said with a smile.

April moved closer and put her arms around Oksana, who in returned did the same thing. The stayed holding each other for quite some time. Others came out to the deck and left, most were couples others were women who met   and wanted a place to quickly make out with each other. Then Jo and her wife comes outside.

"So this is were you two got to." Jo said

'Yes, we wanted to be alone for a while."

"Yeah, these parties can do that to people." Karly says.

"So how have you been Karly, last I talked to you was what a few weeks ago, how's the new job." April asked.

"It's good, thanks for asking, I am sorry to hear about you and your girlfriend."

"Thanks, hey I'm sad about it, but Oksana here is helping me get over Kelly, so I think I'll be good."

A smile came across Oksana's face and she said in Russian "yah fsir' – yos ga va ryu' vlyu bi tsa a-nah" (I'm seriously falling in love with her.)

Jo replied "Really maybe you should tell her."

April looks very confused and says "Wait Jo I've known you since school , when did you learn Russian?" "Oh I guess I never told you, remember our High school English teacher."

"Yeah, why she didn't teach us Russian."

"No April, she privately taught me Russian, when her husband was out of town."

April sounds not to surprised "Dam it I know she was sleeping with a student, but I didn't know it was you."

"Yeah, well after we had sex and dinner she taught me a little Russian, because she knew that Communism was coming to an end."

'No wonder you past her class and she taught us for all four years. I can't believe it you fucked our English teacher and never said anything about it."

"Well she is good at keeping secrets, remember how she is around Christmas, we all go crazy trying to get her to tell." Karly replies.

"Your right" April says then turns to Oksana and ask. "So what did you say."

"I will tell you over breakfast if want."

"Breakfast sounds good."

April and Oksana embrace in lip locking passionate kiss, and forget that anyone else is around.

"So Karly honey, I think we should leave these two alone." Jo says.

"I think your right baby."

So Karly and Jo walk back into the party and disappear into the group of people moving around. After a while Oksana and April come up for air.

"Wow that was great." April said sounding a little out of breathe.

"I agree." Oksana replied and then pressed her lips against Aprils again.

April replied. "Wait." Pulling Oksana off of her

"don't you want me to kiss you." She asked

"Yes, but why don't we blow this party and go back to my place or yours."

"Good idea, mine is closer, it's just down the street."

Oksana and April take each others hand and they leave the party through the back way, none notice that they were gone. They start walking down the street towards Oksana's apartment.

"So how far is it." April asked.

"Not much farther, It's right over there." Okasana said as she pointed to a tall set of buildings that look like they have recently been remodelled. They get to Oksana apartment she types in the security code, and the door clicks open. Oksana moves aside and motions for April to go first.

"Thank you." April says as she brushed by Oksana and enters the lobby.

Oksana follows making sure the door is closed and locked, they both walk towards the elevator. Then once they get in Oksana presses the button to her floor.

"I think you like here." Oksana said as she moves closer to April and takes her hand.

"I think your right." April replies as she turns and faces Oksana and gives her a very passionate kiss that last until the elevator doors open to Oksana's floor. They barely made it out of the elevator before the door closed. Still in each others arms, they walked down the hall and got to Oksana's apartment. Oksana pulled out the keys from her purse and opened the door.   They almost fell in as the door opened.

Closing the door behind them , April stopped and pulled away.

"what's wrong April." Oksana asked.

"Nothing, I'm enjoying this, but I think before one of gets injured that we should just go into the bedroom and get ready, then we start making out again." April replied back.

Oksana smiles, takes April but the hand and leads her into her bedroom. April is amazed how beautiful the bedroom is. The bed has lace motif with and awning over it. With pink and white in the whole mix around the room.

"I love your room, it's beautiful."

'Thank you, now get on the bed, so we can fuck."

April gives Oksana a look the replies. "Boy you don't waste anytime do you."

"No, now get." Oksana says as she moves April to the edge of the bed and pushes her down.

April complies and she moves to the centre of the bed. Seconds later Oksana gets on to the bed, she then moves on to April and starts to unbutton April's dress, and slowly slipped down it her shoulders. April was not wearing a bra but she did have a pair of black silk thong panties with a matching garter belt that were connected to a pair of spider wed style nylons. Oksana sat there on top of April staring at her beautiful semi naked body.

"What?" April asked looking up at Oksana.

"Nothing, you are very beautiful." Oksana replied.

April started to blush a little, then she pulled Oksana close to her and started to kiss her. Oksana returned the kiss then she moved her right hand down April's bare skin, stopping at her breast and rubbing April's erect nipples with her fingers. A shiver of sexual pleasure ran through Aprils body with each touch.

"Oh, yes Oksana fuck me?" April moaned

Oksana move her mouth towards Aprils left ear and whispered "With Pleasure honey." Then she moved down Aprils body. Sucking on her nipples as she goes down, reaching the top edge of the panties and garter, Oksana takes the top of the panties into her teeth and slowly moves then down April's leg. Oksana takes a whiff of April's sweet juices. She finishes removing the panties from Aprils body. Oksana moves back up sticking her head between April's legs, and she lightly takes her tongue and touches April's clit with it. Another pleasurable shiver goes through April's Body, she squirms as Oksana continues to play with April's clit. April grabs the brass bed poles tight as she gets Oksana going down on her.

Moments later Oksana lifts her head and says "Ne konchay" in Russian (Don't Come.)

"Oh, god that word I do know, but I don't think I can stop it, I want to cum." April shout in between taking breathes.

"Nyet!"

"Oh god please I want to cum?" April finishes as she grabs her tits and pulls on her own nipple.

At that moment Oksana put her head back down and began to lick April's labia and her erect clit. April screamed out more with pleasure, she grabbed the side of the bed this time and wrapped her feet around Oksana's back, and without a second notice she hit her orgasm and squirted into Oksana's mouth and all over her face and soaking the sheets. Oksana lifted her head up licked her lips and then licked some of the juices from April's pussy.

"Oh wow, I didn't know you squirt."

"Oh, yes I squirt really bad, I end up ruining sheets."

"Great I love women who cum, I love tasting their juices in my mouth and down my mouth." Oksana said as she climbed up next to April and shared a small kiss with her.

"I like you Oksana" April said as she put her arm around her.

"I like you too."

They both cuddle for a while until they fell asleep in each others arms, and stayed that way until the morning, when Oksana woke to the smell of breakfast cooking.

Chapter Three

April and Oksana are sitting across from each other in Sasha and Kelly's dining room, the four of them have become good friends in the last few months, since April has met Oksana. They are eating a large meal that was prepared by Kelly and April, who has never revealed that Kelly had an affair with April to Sasha. A secret that they are hoping will always remain a secret.

"So how is dinner ladies?" Kelly asks

Sasha looks at Kelly with a smile and replies "It's wonderful honey, I just love it."

Oksana nods and says "I agree, It is great, the best I have had in a while."

"Well wait till we get to desert. " April says lightly kicking Oksana under the table.

"Desert, wow I can hardly wait. Sasha said as she looks across at Kelly.

Kelly gives Sasha a blushing smile and replied "Yes, it took a few hours to cook."

Kelly and April get up , putting their napkins on their plates and they both walk towards the kitchen. April brushes up against Kelly. Kelly turns and gives a small smile. Then she goes to the fridge opens it up and pulls out a large white frosted cake.

"Do you think Sasha will like it." Kelly asked.

"Yes, for the last time Yes, she will like it, you spent a good part of the day making it and getting the Cyrillic writing right on it. " April said helping Kelly with the cake.

They walk out into the dining room both carrying the cake.

"Here you go, a white frosting lemon flavoured cake." April said as they sat it on the table.." April said as they sat it on the table.

You wrote it honey didn't you?" Sasha asked.

"Yes, why did I get it wrong?" Kelly sounded worried

"Oh no , you spelled it right, I just surprised that you took the time to do it." Sasha got up and gave Kelly a hug and a kiss. Then she adds "I love you"

"I love you too." Kelly replied.

Then Oksana gets up and walks over to April and wraps her arms around April. "You that was a nice think to do, Do you know what it says." Oksana asked.

"No not really, when we were making it , Kelly kept the Russian book away from me." April answered.

"well in that case dear, it's real simple." She puts her head on April's shoulder and finishes " It says Happy Birthday, My Love."

"Thanks, I have been with you for three months now, and I still can get a hold of the Russian language." April says sounding disappointed.

"Don't sound sad honey learning Our language is hard, since it's not a Latin based language." Oksana said.

"Thank you, that helps." April says as she leans over and gives Oksana a kiss. Then they turn and face Kelly and Sasha and she adds. "Happy Birthday Sasha"

"Thank you April and Oksana for the wonderful gift?" Sasha said as she walked over to the two women, then she added "I know now who I want to be my maid of honour at our wedding, and it's you April."

"Thanks, I would love to be your maid of honour but Kelly had already asked me."

"Oh I should have realized, but not to make a bad choice, and I would like it to stay as couple, so would you like to Oksana."

Oksana stood there for a second and then replied. "I would love to, I have never been a maid of Honour or anything at a wedding, but a guess."

"Well there you go sweaty we'll have a fun time, especially planning the bachelorette parties."

"Oh one thing about that April, nothing to weird, and remember two of our friends still can't be in same room with each other."

"I'll keep that all in mind."

All four women gave each other a hug and friendly kisses. Then they headed to the living room and sat down to have tea and cake. They sat and talked for hours, only stopping to fill the tea pot a few times. Then Sasha looked at her watch.

"Oh wow, its already 1030 at night< I like to thank you all this was a wonderful birthday party, but I must head upstairs, I have an early client tomorrow." Sasha gets up and heads up stairs.

"I'll be there in a minute sweat heart." Kelly yelled up.

April and Oksana got up from the couch and gave Kelly a hug. They all walked over to the door.

"So I'll see you later then" Kelly said as she opened the door.

"Yeah I have to plan your party." April replied as she took Oksana's hand and walked out the door.

Kelly shut the door. Locked it and made sure all the lights were off before she headed up stairs. Walking to the bedroom, Sasha was already In bed when Kelly walked into the bedroom .

"are you asleep baby." Kelly asked

Sasha rolled over and replied "No but I am tired."

"Are you mad"

"No but You should have said that April would be your brides maid." Sasha said in a disappointing voice.

Kelly removes most of her clothes leaving her bra and panties on then she climbed into bed and wrapped her arm around Sasha.

"I'm sorry, I can always change if you want, I don't want you to be angry with me."

"I'm not, I want you to be happy and if having her as your brides maid makes you happy, then I am fine with that." Sasha says as she moves and gets on top of Kelly and gives her a kiss.

Kelly kisses her back and started to move her hand down Sasha's back and started to remove her sweatshirt that she was wearing to bed. Once Sasha had her shirt off exposing her breast and pressing them against Kelly's breast that are still in her bra, that Sasha is trying to unlatch from the back.

"Honey, stop it unhooks from the front." Kelly says in Sasha's ear.

"Oh thanks baby." Sasha squeezes her hand in between her and Kelly's breast, then unlatches the clasp and removes the bra. They kiss some more and Kelly reaches down and removes her panties with Sasha's help.

"I love you Sasha with all my heart, I don't want anything to come between us."

"I know and thanks to Cassandra I know we'll grow old together."

"That would make me happy.

"I am glad that does, it makes me happy also."

The two women kiss again, and now Sasha has moved her hand down between Kelly's legs, and started to figure Kelly's swollen clit.

"oh wow, I love it when you do that baby." Kelly moaned.

"I know, I want to please you tonight, no commands just lay back and enjoy it."

"Yes my dear." Kelly finished as she adjusted her self on the bed under Sasha.

Sasha continued to kiss Kelly as she moved her mouth down on her chin, then on to Kelly's neck. Stopping along the shoulders, giving April love bites. Then Sasha continued down kissing between her breast and then she did something that surprised Kelly, instead of kissing, or even teasing her nipples somewhat, Sasha just continued down not even stopping at Kelly's belly piercing. Sasha moved along Kelly's outer thigh of her right leg, then jumping over to her left leg and up the thigh. Kelly was wonder what Sasha was doing, until she felt Sasha's warm breathe hovering over her left nipple and then with no warning Sasha took a very hard but pleasurable bite of the nipple, making Kelly squirm and moan each time Sasha took a bite.

"Oh god, my nipple is so sensitive please don't stop." Kelly continued to moan.

Sasha sucked a little harder as Kelly continued the moan in pleasure. Then Sasha stopped and looked at Kelly smiled, nodded then said "I want us to be fuck."

Kelly smiled back and nodded. They both moved around on the bed, they sat at oppiste ends of the bed and faced each other Sasha spread her legs first and moved a little closer to Kelly. Kelly then spread her legs and met with Sasha, their came close and then their inner lips touched. They began to move a little and rub their pussies together. Both women began to moan in unison.

"Oh god yes, I love it when we fuck like this." Kelly says as they rub faster and faster.

Sasha grabs on to Kelly's leg and pulls as she moans in pleasure. Kelly starts to play with Sasha's feet trying to suck on her toes as they continue to fuck. They continues for a good twenty minutes, having small orgasms that would nock an average women out of the bed, but not to these two, their bodies compliment each others orgasms and they can even come together which actually happens a lot especially in the tribadism position. They continue to fuck even after their many orgasm's wanting a bigger one and it came.

"Oh fuck I'm coming Sasha." Kelly screamed.

"Wait for me, I want to cum with you." Sasha said in between the moaning.

Then with no warning Sasha started to squirt her juices and then Kelly started to squirt. They shared each others juices cover each other. Once they were completely finished, they sat in the position, and rubbed their juices over themselves and tasting it a couple of time.

Kelly speaking as she tries to recover her breathe. "I love you Sasha with all of my heart. I want to get married sooner then a few months."

Sasha sat up with her elbows bracing her and replied "I do too, I love you and what ever will make you happy, my love."

Sasha sat all the way up, helping Kelly up they faced each other and then they started to kiss. Getting closer again their whole bodies touched and rubbed against each other. Their hands started to explore each others bodies they then pulled apart from each other and sat on the bed looking at each other. Sasha got up and started to leave the room when Kelly got up and stopped her.

"honey where are you going." Kelly asked

Sasha turning around and looking at Kelly she replied "I'm just heading to the bathroom, I'll be right back."

Kelly smiled letting go of Sasha's arm and then heading back to the bed. Kelly got under the covers waiting for Sasha to return. Moments later Sasha comes walking back in, turning off the light and then walking over to the bed and sitting on the edge of the bed.

"What's the matter." Kelly said as she sat up a little and put her hand on Sasha's back.

Sasha turns to face Kelly and replies "Are you sure you want to marry me?"

Kelly sits completely up no holding Sasha in both arms. " Yes I'm sure baby, I love you and nothing can take that away, I will love you until the end of days. , why would you ask such a thing."

"There were these anti-gay protestors outside of city hall today when I was there, and they said that gays shouldn't be able to marry or even hold down jobs."

Kelly holding Sasha tighter "Honey don't pay attention to then, they are arrogant self absorb bastards, that think the world revolves around them and they want everyone to think they way they do and obey them, I love you and I wouldn't worry about them."

"Your right, I'm sorry I've been acting strange for a couple of days, lets get some sleep okay."

"Okay"

They both get under the covers and hold each other until they both fell asleep. The next morning Sasha and Kelly awoke at the same time, to the door bell. Kelly slowly gets up and grabs their robes, putting one and handing the other to

Sasha. Kelly followed by Sasha walk down the stairs as the door bell rings again.

"Alright already we're coming." Kelly said

"Who the hell would be ringing the doorbell this early." Sasha asked.

"I don't know?" Kelly replied back and then got to the door and looked out the side window by the door and added. "Oh god no it's my mother, what the hell."

"She's probably here to help for our wedding."

The door bell rang once more, then Sasha opened it with Kelly standing behind the door. Kelly's mother smiled as she walked past Sasha and into the living room.

"Well hello Sasha how is everything, oh I see that your not dressed, what a shame lost another job."

"Mrs. Walberg " Sasha said just as Kelly popped out from behind the door.

"Mother so nice to see you, what are you doing here."

Kelly's mother walks over to Kelly and fixes her hair then replies. "I came to help you two with your wedding, I only have one daughter, and even if she is a lesbian I'm not going to miss her wedding."

"Oh mum, I love you."

Kelly moves and gives her mother a hug. Then Mrs Walberg waved for Sasha to join them. Sasha walked over and now all three women were embraced in a hug.

"Okay, I do have to get ready for work though." Sasha said as she broke a way from the hug and went back up stairs.

"So is she okay, what does she do." Mrs Walberg asked.

"Mom, don't start, she has a nice career at a good law firm."

"Hey I just to make sure that the women my daughter is marrying will support her and my future grandchildren."

"Mom, we haven't even talked about children nor who would carry them."

"Oh honey it would have to be you, your feminine then Sasha."

"Mom stop, or I'll take you to a hotel until the wedding."

"Fine, I'll be on my best behaviour."

"That would be a first."

"And what is that suppose to mean little one."

Kelly shouting at the top of her lungs as she walks away 'just remember what happened at my brother Josephs wedding, I can't believe you did that."

"Hey I'm sorry but no bride should be wearing a slip as her brides made dress."

Kelly stops and turns around. "Mum they had a sleep over still wedding, everyone was in pj's or lingerie."

Mrs. Walberg stops and thinks for a minute. "oh, that makes more sense now."

"mom I don't know what to do with you."

"I do where am I going to stay."

"Mom well here of course, you can have the spare room, it's up stairs on the right just before our bedroom."

"wait you two sleep in the same bed"

"Mom don't act surprised, we love each other, and that what people do."

"Not what I mean, your sleeping together before your wedding."

"Well yeah,"

"and having sex."

Kelly starts to blush. "Mom, non of your business."

"Ok I'll compromise,, you two can stay in the same bed, but promise me that you'll save yourself for your wedding night."

"Mom"

"Promise me.

Kelly walks closer to her mother takes her hand and says "okay I promise, I'll tell Sasha as soon as she gets out of the shower."

'Thank you" Mrs. Walberg finishes as she give Kelly a kiss on the cheek.

Kelly walks upstair caring her mothers luggage into the spare room. She places it on the bed and then leaves heading to her room where she waits for Sasha to walk in. Kelly sits on the bed and then a few minutes later Sasha walks in closing the door.

"okay what's with the long face honey." Sasha said as she came closer to Kelly throwing her towel down and then sitting on the bed next to her, putting her arm around Kelly.

"DON'T" Kelly said removing Sasha's arm from her shoulder.

"Okay what the hell is the matter, your mother shows up and you get ice cold."

Kelly shakes her head "no it's nothing like that, I promised my mother that if we still sleep in the same room, that we wouldn't have sex until after the wedding.

Sasha stands up and starts mumbling something in Russian, then she says. "How dare her coming into our house and make demands on you."

"Honey come sit, at least we still get to hold each other and cuddle."

"Yes I guess."

"And if we are really quiet we can sneak in some sex, like that movie you like watching so much.

"Oh yeah, Better Then Chocolate, I love that movie, especially when the girls give up their room to Karen Drwyers characters mother and they end up having sex on the couch ."

'yes exactly.'

"Cool I can live with that, or we can go and have sex in a public bathroom."

Kelly stands up. "I don't think so" she says, then walks out of the bedroom.

Kelly walks back down stairs where her mother has begun cleaning the house. She walks into the living room and sits down on the couch. Mrs. Walberg stops vacuuming walks over and sits next to her daughter.

"What's wrong honey, did Sasha not go for the idea." Mrs. Walberg asked

"No, she did go for the idea, which I was hoping she wouldn't."

"Why"

"Because mum, I love her and for the last few months our relationship has been like a roller coaster, we even went to go see a relationship specialist."

Mrs. Walberg gives her daughter a hug and replies. "You two love each other right."

"Yes."

"That is all that matters, you two seem happy together, do you remember the day you came home in high school and told your father and me that you were a lesbian and introduced us to your girlfriend."

"How can I forget, I was so nervous, my mind was racing with a million thoughts."

"And we still loved you then, and we didn't like it, but it was you and you are who you are, we knew that. So I guess what I am saying is forget what I asked, just do what you and your brother did when you guys had your girlfriends over."

Kelly gives her mother a small smile and a hug "Thanks Mom."

Kelly gets off the couch and runs back up the stairs to her bedroom. Swings open the door and jumps into Sasha's arms knocking both on to the bed.

"what is that for." Sasha asked as she wrapped her arms around Kelly.

"Forget what I promised mom, all we have to do is keep the noise down." Kelly said as she frantically began kissing Sasha, then she added "I love you."

"I love you too." Sasha replies trying to get Kelly to stop.

"Honey I want to have lunch with you today." Kelly asked as she moved her self off of Sasha.

"That would be wonderful, come to the firm around one pm."

Kelly gets off the bed and helps Sasha up as she finishes "Great I'll be there ."

Kelly and Sasha walk down the stairs, Kelly's mother is standing at the bottom of the stairs. Holding a camera and she takes a few pictures of the two girls.

"This reminds me of Kelly's prom night."

"Oh really, you must tell me, she won't say any thing about her high school girlfriends, Mrs. Walberg."

"I'll tell you the whole story over dinner tonight, and please call me Hannah, you already family."

"Thank you, but I must go now." Sasha says giving Kelly a kiss and then leaving out the front door.

Kelly walks over to her mother in a day dream state and then gives Hannah a look.

"What I think you and Paige looked very cute in your prom dresses."

'Thanks mom, she doesn't know that Paige and I dated in High school, and she never really asked."

"So what do you have to be afraid of, she loves you, you can see it, come I made you some breakfast."

Kelly and her mother walk into the kitchen and eat the breakfast that Hannah had made. After that they cleaned up and went shopping at the Alderwood Mall. Walking around from store to store. They stopped in at Victoria Secrets. A young lady approached them and began helping them look for nice sexy lingerie that Kelly and Sasha would both enjoy. Mother and daughter walked around the mall for a few hours until Kelly needed to get ready for her lunch date.

"Okay dear, now remember you two need to be home tonight, I'm making dinner"

"Okay mum, I'm just having lunch, it's not like I'm going to a hotel and having sex."

"Thanks I really needed to know that."

"I'm kidding mum, will be okay getting home from here."

"yes dear, I'll be fine."

Kelly gives her mom a hug and leaves her at the mall. She drives back to Seattle, finds a parking spot near Sasha's law firm. Kelly locks the car and walks into the front of the building and up to the receptionist desk The receptionist looks up and at Kelly.

"How can I help you Miss."

"I'm here to Sasha Harrington"

"Do you have an appointment"

"No, I'm her lunch date."

'Oh I see one of those people."

Kelly stands firm and stares right at the receptionist and says "One of what people may I ask."

The receptionist goes back typing as she replied. "You know, a person that is against god, and everything he holds to truth, you are a sinner miss and you will die in hell."

"Oh really, well I didn't ask what you thought or your opinion, So do your damn job and get Sasha Harrington now."

"Don't take that tone with me you dyke, or I will call security."

"If you do that I'll have you fired."

Just as Kelly and the receptionist where about to get into it a security guard walks over .

"Is there a problem here." He says.

Kelly turns and recognizes the guards "Yes, I'm here for a lunch date with my girlfriend and this bitch gets all holy on me."

The receptionist stands up "Bitch who are you call a bitch lesbo."

Kelly was just about to reach over the desk but the security guard stopped her.

"let go George, I'm going to kick her ass."

"No your not Kelly, I'm escorting you up to Sasha's office."

The receptionist goes back to typing on the. George takes Kelly over to the elevator, presses the button and waits for the door to open, not once letting go of Kelly.

"Sorry about her Kelly, but she's new"

"I don't care if she the owners daughter, she has no right talking to me like that, I'm telling Sasha."

"Good, you are not the only one she's done that to, you know Mr. Peterson."

"Yeah, why"

"Well the first day she started it seems that she accused him of being a panhandler and tried to get him thrown out of here."

"Oh good, she's not only homophobic, but a racist too."

The elevator doors open and as Kelly and George step in Kelly turn and screams "You're the one going to hell."

George lets Kelly go to Sasha's office unaccompanied, some of Sasha's co-workers wave and she waves back, she finally gets to Sasha's office, but Sasha is no where to be seen. She walks over and sit in her chair behind the desk and spins it around. A couple of people walk by and look in at Kelly having fun. Then without any warning or Kelly knowing Sasha stands in the doorway.

"Um, having fun honey?"

Kelly stops the chair at looks at her girlfriend, she puts on a I'm cute smile and replies. "Hi, are you ready."

"I will be in just a second, oh I heard you had a run in with our new receptionist."

"Yes she is really mean, I don't like her, I think you should fire her."

"I would honey, put she is the daughter of one of my partners, and every time we confront her about her actions she plays this dumb blonde routine, so we keep her on, and we actually don't pay her anything, this job is credits for college course."

"In what being a bitch."

"No, but I will be right back, and then we can go, oh don't touch anything."

Sasha walks away from her office and down the hall, Kelly looks around and then starts to opens the desk drawers. She finds paper clips, staples, a glass, even a small bottle of Russian Vodka. Then she opens the bottom drawer and finds a vibrator.

Thinking to her self "Now why would she need this here when she has a few at home, and me for that matter."

Kelly hears Sasha walking back and quickly puts everything back and closes the drawers. Then she sits straight up at the desk acting like a good little girl. Sasha walks in and gives Kelly a strange look.

"What, I was being good." Kelly says with a sinister smile.

"Yeah that would be the first."

"Hey, if I didn't love you so much, I would take that as an insult."

"Yeah what ever are you ready."

Kelly gets up from Sasha's desk walks over to Sasha and grabs her arm.

"I am now lets go."

Kelly and Sasha walk down the hall to the elevator, when a man approaches them.

"hey Donald what's up"

"Don't for get we have that court appearance this afternoon." Donald said.

'I won't I'll only be gone for about an hour, Oh have you met my girlfriend."

Donald shakes his head and holds out his hand. "Hi I'm Donald Stevens a new attorney here."

"Nice to meet you my name is Kelly."

"So I'll see you about two thirty then Donald."

"Gotcha."

Kelly and Sasha get in to the elevator and head to the parking garage. Kelly gets into her car followed by Sasha. They drive off towards their favourite restaurant. The Japanese Bistro that is located on Harbour Steps.

"So can you talk about work, today." Kelly asked

"No not really, I can tell you after the case is over, so lets talk about something else okay."

Kelly moves her free hand over to Sasha's and replies "okay sweaty, so what do you want to talk about."

"Well what about your family, is your brother coming to the wedding?" Sasha asked

"I really don't think so, I did talk to him early in the week though, his wife doesn't think its right for me being a lesbian to have the same rights as her, so he said if he did show it would be just him, I don't even get to see my niece and nephew."

"That sad, that people still think that way, I feel sorry for them."

"I don't I never really liked her, she didn't even want me at her wedding, my brother had to twist her arm to let me come."

"I think we should find another subject to talk about."

"Okay that sounds good to me Sasha."

They arrive by the Harbour Steps and find a place to park the Crossfire. Sasha takes Kelly's hand and they walk up to the restaurant. A young Japanese woman dressed in a floral style Kimono greats them at the door. They walked in and got a seat by the window, so that they could watch all the people walking around the steps on a sunny day in Seattle. The waitress placed two menus down in front of Kelly and Sasha, then left. A few minutes later she returned with two glasses of water then asked them if they were ready to order. Kelly ordered her meal followed by Sasha, the waitress left after getting their order.

"Okay so how bad is your mother going to help us with our wedding." Sasha asked after taking a sip of water.

'I don't think she'll try to do to much, my mum has no experience with trying to plan a lesbian wedding, so I think she'll just give us suggestions and try to help us without to much being a mother."

"good, I love your mother, but she is an expert at being a mother especially when her daughter is getting married."

The waitress begins them their food and sets it down in front of them , nods and then leaves. Kelly looks at Sasha's plate and takes a piece of her teriyaki chicken and eats it.

"Hey, that was mine."

"Not anymore, you're a lawyer you should know that this is a equal marriage state, even for lesbians."

"yes I know, but I don't think that would apply to our lunch." Sasha commented.

They ate lunch and even had dessert. Kelly drove Sasha back to her office, walked into the lobby with her seeing the receptionist, Kelly took Sasha's hand as they walked by the desk and then gave Sasha a big kiss on the lips. The receptionist sneered and then went back to her typing.

Sasha glanced at the receptionist and once Kelly was done, she pulled away. They finished walking to the elevator.

"You did that on purpose." Sasha said

"Yes I did, I don't like her"

"Kelly behave, besides I think she's in the closet."

"How, she totally says hateful things about everyone"

"How else would hide how you really feel."

"I guess." Kelly finishes .

The elevator doors open and Sasha gives Kelly one last kiss before she gets in. "I'll see you at home honey." Sasha says as the doors close.

Kelly walks past the receptionist, she looks up from the computer and Kelly winks. Kelly leaves and heads home. Once she pulls in the drive way, there is a strange car there. She gets out locks her car and heads to the house, but before she can get there, two young children come running out of the door. It is her niece and nephew, followed but her brother and sister in law. The children ran over and gave her a hug.

"wow this is a surprise."

"Hi auntie Kel." Christian said.

"Hi guys, okay you can stop now."

The children hugged her a little tighter and then let go. She took the kids hands and walked over to her brother, who walked part of the way and gave her a hug.

"Hi sis how's it going." Steven said as she hugged him back.

"I'm so clad you're here, and you brought the family."

Whispers in her ear "well don't tell mom, but she blacked mailed Rebecca into coming and being nice."

"We'll that does sound like mom, but I'm still glad you're here."

"Hey I wouldn't miss my baby sisters wedding."

"Thank you"

She puts her arm around his shoulder and the head towards the house. Rebecca walks up and holds out her hand to shake with Kelly. Kelly takes her hand and gives Rebecca a shake.

"Well I am glad to see you sister in law."

"I'm sure it is" Rebecca said in a semi mean voice.

"Alright, lets go inside and catch up on things, shall we kids." Hannah said

They all walked inside the house and sat in the living room talking all through the rest of the day. When Sasha came home she was introduced to Steven's wife and children, which the children seemed really happy with Sasha and they played with her until Hannah said that it was time for dinner. Rebecca kept quiet for most of the evening even when they brought up the story of Steven and Kelly's prom. Rebecca took the children and went to the room to put the children down to sleep, so she wouldn't have to answer any of the questions about their aunt marrying another woman. So for the next few days they all seemed the normal dysfunctional happy American family. But when the prep for the wedding started it seemed that Rebecca became her normal hating self.

Chapter Four

Everyone is asleep and for once in Sasha and Kelly's relationship their house is full of family. Sasha's brother Boris and father also showed up a couple of days ago. Sasha and Kelly are asleep on the floor in the den. Giving Kelly's brother and sister in law their king size bed. Kelly is the first to wake up. She quietly unzips her half of the sleeping bag and gently gets up, realizing that her Ipod was still in the sleeping bag. She picks it up and sticks it on speaker/charger unit on the table. Looking around and sees how beautiful her future wife is asleep. Kelly puts on her robe and heads to the kitchen where her brother already is making coffee.

Steven turns around and sees that Kelly is walking into the kitchen. "Good morning sis, how are you doing."

"I'm okay, how is your wife doing after last night."

"Well she seems fine, but she's still asleep. With the twins."

"I am so sorry, about that."

Steven walks over and gives Kelly a hug and finishes the conversation by saying "Sis it's not your fault nor is it Sasha's this is your house and you two are a couple, Rebecca has to come to terms with that."

"thank you, so you still haven't told me how mum blackmailed Rebecca."

"No I haven't, want some coffee."

"no thanks, I drink tea remember."

Steven nods his head and pulls a pitcher of hot water "yes I do hot water for you and Sasha, who I assume is still sleeping too."

"Yeah, she likes to camp, so sleeping on the floor is just as good as sex."

"I very much doubt that remember my room was next to yours , sis I could always hear you making out with your girlfriends."

Kelly starts to blush as she walks over and sits down at the breakfast table. Steven brings over the coffee and hot water. After he places them on the table he goes back to the stove island and brings pancakes bacon and toast.

"here I made breakfast for every one in the house." Steven said as he sat down next to Kelly. Then a few minutes later Sasha comes wondering in still rubbing here eyes.

Kelly stands up and walks over to her "Good morning honey" and then gives her a morning kiss on the lips.

"Good morning, what's so good about it, it's a Saturday and I'm awake before ten o'clock."

"I know but we have a full house, come have some tea and breakfast." Kelly adds as she takes Sasha's hand and leads her to the table. They both sit down and then all three start eating breakfast. All is well until Rebecca comes walking into the kitchen. All three of them look up from breakfast. Kelly gets up wipes her face and then walks over to Rebecca.

"Come join us for breakfast sister."

'Thanks but no thanks, Steven I want to go now."

"Becka we talked about this, my sister is getting married and I want to be there."

"Steven think of your family, I am your wife , and besides this wedding should never have become legal, they are a sin against god."

"Now wait a minute Rebecca, she is my sister and I love her, I am staying."

"well if you stay then I want a divorce my children will not grow up now some queers in the family."

"Then give my son a divorce and you will never get any claim to my inheritance, and don't think for a minute you would get custody of the children missy." Hannah said standing behind Rebecca.

Rebecca turns around and looks at Hannah "oh won't I their my children"

"Yes But they have my families last name, and in this city our name goes far."

Rebecca huffed back up the stairs and into the room. Steven gets up and follows her and so does Hannah.

"God I can't believe she would act like that in our house." Kelly said then she added. 'I knew that she didn't like me because she knew I was a lesbian, but I was hoping she would get past that."

"Well honey it seems that she did not get past it." Sasha says as she takes a sip of coffee.

"maybe I should go and talk with her, Paige has train ed me in some negotiation tactic lately."

'I doubt if the would work, honey but if you want to give it a try." Sasha finished.

Kelly gets up from the table and heads up to the bedroom and knocks on the door. Her mother opens it up.

"Hi I wanted to know if I could just have a talk with Rebecca, alone."

"I don't see why not, Steven come."

Steven and Hannah leave the room. Kelly walks in closing the door.

'Rebecca just listen and don't say a word. I am sorry that you can't except who I am , I don't really care if you ever do." Kelly says and then she pauses and continues. "I have tried to be civilized and now for you to come in to my house that Sasha and I have worked hard to buy and insult us like that, that is really uncalled for."

Rebecca is looking around the room but never at Kelly.

"Oh my god, I just realized it, why your acting this way."

Rebecca looks directly at Kelly and says "Oh really what is it then."

"Your had a crush on a girl in the past and she turned you down, and now to get back at her you act all holy."

"Yeah well if you think your so smart, explain how I fell in love with your brother."

"Oh that's simple everyone loves my brother he just has that thing about him, and you would be the first girl that was straight and had a crush on girl and became devastated when she didn't return the affection."

Rebecca comes closer and says 'I so loved her, and she left me with no word or any thing." The she starts to cry.

Kelly walks over to her and puts Rebecca's head on her shoulder and pats the back of her head.

"There there Rebecca its fine, do you want to talk about it more." Kelly says as she moves over to the bed and sit down on the edge.

Rebecca nods her head yes and then begins to say. "It all started back in junior high, I had this huge crush on this girl in my class, we had gym and lunch and even a few classes together, so one day I decided to write her a letter and when I saw her in locker room, I stuck it in her backpack. "

'Oh wow, I'm sorry what happened." Kelly asked.

"well she read the letter and laugh about with her friends, I was so embarrassed, that I wanted to change schools, and that when I knew that I would never let that happen to me again."

"But why do you fight so hard against what rights every one wants in life."

"Because not to long after High school I saw that girl that I had a crush on , and she was seeing another woman."

"Oh god, so she turn out to like girls after all, and that must have just crushed you.'

'yes , so then I decided to be hateful towards all to get back at her.'

Kelly putting her arm around her and hugging Rebecca, "Well sis you don't have to be like that, we all had a similar situation like that, and we have come through. It's hard to deal with your first crush and have it blow up in your face. "

"Thank you, I can't believe I told you, I have never told that story to anyone."

"opening up helps us understand who we really are, and besides we aren't all that evil."

Rebecca gives a smile. Kelly smiles back then adds 'I know what how would you like to be in my wedding as another brides maid."

"I don't know, Kelly I've been mean to you and your girlfriend, why"

"Oh come on, you can show off that what she did to you doesn't hurt anymore, and besides you don't want to divorce my brother, you two are perfect together, and besides I would never get to see his hot looking wife anymore."

Rebecca started to blush and then responded. "You think I'm hot"

'hell yeah, you want to know something that I've never told anyone."

"Sure"

Kelly moves in closer and whispers in Rebecca's ear. "We'll when he first met you and you guys would have sex in his bed room at home when our parents weren't home, I would listen to the well and masterbate each time you would moan and pretend that I was having sex with you."

"Really, wow, how where we."

"Oh we were great."

Kelly and Rebecca shared another hug, just as there was a knock on the door.

"yes" Kelly and Rebecca answered in unison.

The door slowly crept opened , standing there was Hannah, Steven and Sasha. "Well we didn't hear anything, and was just wondering who killed who." Steven said

Rebecca stands and replies 'No one we talked and Kelly has made me one of her maids of honour."

All three stand in the doorway speechless, and they look at each other not believing what Rebecca just said.

"that's right, I made her one of my maids of honour." Kelly said as she walks over towards Sasha.

Kelly and Sasha put their arms around each other, and then Rebecca went over to Steven and gave him a hug.

"Okay what did you and my sister talk about. Steven asked.

Rebecca and Kelly look at each other and Rebecca replies. "That's between Kelly and I, right"

"Right" Kelly adds.

"okay, as long as we can get a long."

Kelly takes Rebecca's arm and says "okay so it's a girls day out, sorry Sasha and Steven no spouses"

They head down stairs and out the door.

Sasha and Steven shrug their shoulders. "Okay what just happened here."

Hannah says "Well they did what we all wanted they seem to be getting along now."

The rest of the family goes about their business, as Kelly and Rebecca are in Kelly's crossfire driving towards Seattle.

"So where are we going Kelly " I figured that we could spend some time walking around Seattle and then we could get to know more of each other, and if you don't mind I would like to hear more of the girl who broke your heart and her name."

"Sure, but I don't see why, in the long run she wasn't that great to be around." Rebecca said in a soft tone.

"I figured that, but I would like to help you get that bad image out of your head, and show that not all of us are like that." Kelly replies.

"Okay, but how do you plan on doing that without getting us in trouble with your brother or Sasha."

"We are just going to the waterfront and talk, I know this place by the maritime museum that no one will bother us and we can watch the ships on the sound."

"sounds okay, I guess."

They arrive in Seattle by the waterfront, and Kelly finds a parking spot not to far from the museum and the park. They walked across the street to the sidewalk by the park, Kelly takes Rebecca by the arm and they walk up the stairs and sit next to one of the sculptures in the park.

"So tell me more about this girl"

"Well like I said before she was a very pretty girl, at least I thought so in school, she had strawberry blonde hair, and the cutest little dimples that showed up when she smiled. And the unforgettable laugh that would make anyone melt."

"So then after you told her that you liked her, and she blew you off, and then come to find out that she did start dating woman, did you ever confront her."

"I couldn't she was at the same college when I say her with a woman."

"Oh, that doesn't mean anything she could have been a LUG."

"A LUG, what is a LUG"

"A college turn used by people, that see women only dating women in college, it stands for lesbian until graduation, even though a few of them actually stay on my team and don't go back, So what was her name."

'Oh lets see if I can remember it. Oh yeah it was Amanda Connors, but I think she was going by"

Kelly interrupts Rebecca "Sinclair"

"Yes, you know her."

"I might do you know what she does for a living now."

'Yes I believe she is a assistant DA for Seattle."

"Holy fuck, yes I do know her, she is one of our best friends, and so is her ex Paige Sinclair."

Rebecca just stares blankly into Kelly's face, and then she says. "Oh, well I would like to meet her and see if she remembers me."

'You not mad."

'For what, you didn't know, and I have to confront this, so I can move on and not have my children hating me, because I refuse to let them hang out with their aunt Kelly."

'Okay I believe I can make an arrangement for you to meet, since she's not seeing any one anymore, it shouldn't be that hard to drag her out to dinner."

"that sounds good, so then we would have to figure out how to get away from our spouses."

"Oh that wouldn't be to hard, I will just tell Sasha that I'm meeting Amanda for dinner , and that she wants to talk."

"Wait she won't ask anything else."

"No, she and I have this trust thing, and besides she doesn't really like Amanda all that much, not after what she did to Paige."

"really so they must be good friends."

"Yes they new each other with a couple of our other friends in since elementary."

"Oh wow."

"so your fine with all of this now."

"Yeah, I'll be alright. I just have to get used to all of this again."

"what do you mean again you have my brother and two wonderful children."

" Well, don't get upset but when I started dating your brother, I kind of started to feel that way towards you."

Kelly has a surprised look on her face. "You mean you had a crush on me."

Rebecca nods her head "Yeah, just a little one, but so it wouldn't go anywhere, I kept inside and became very angry with you also."

"I didn't know, you could have always came and talked with me."

Rebecca moves closer on the bench and adds "I didn't want to get hurt, like I did back in high school."

'I would have never done that. You were dating my brother and I was not seeing any one at the time."

Rebecca begins to look confused "I don't understand"

"Well it's not like I have never slept with any of my brothers girlfriends before, and I still don't think he knows about any of that."

"I don't know what to say."

'Don't say anything, It could never happen now, so before anything starts I don't want you to get hurt, so can only be friends. But I think you should tell Steven that you also like women, and then maybe your relationship with him can be fixed."

"You think I should, you don't think we would get into a fight."

"No, if any thing I know my brother, he will be fine with it, because he would see that you are excepting of his sister and her girlfriend."

"okay then I'll do it once we get home, you can make the dinner arrangements and I'll talk with Steven and tell him everything is fine between you and me."

"Sounds good ready to go?"

"I guess, I just love this park, it's really cool." Rebecca finishes as she looks around. Then she gets up and walks around on the grass and then onto the walk way over the train tracks.

Followed by Kelly who walks close to her sister in law. They head back to Kelly's car. Then once they get in Kelly pulls out and they head home. They were silent on the way home, but Kelly was thinking to her self that this has been an enemy of her sister in law is now becoming friends with her, and they know a little about each other that no one knows, so it can't be all that bad. It seems her sister in law really is sincere of mending a broken relationship, so she'll give her the benefit of the doubt. About twenty minutes later they get back to Kelly's house, and once they both get out of the car, it seems the whole family was waiting peaking through the window. The door opens and Sasha was standing in the door way .

"Oh thank god you're okay honey I was hoping she didn't do anything to you " Sasha says as she gives Kelly a hug.

"Yes I am fine, why would she do anything to me, or I to her." Kelly replied trying to break away from the hug.

Rebecca is greeted by Steven as she says "Steven I need to talk with you in private, lets go up to our room."

Steven gave a confused look but replied "Okay, I guess."
Steven and Rebecca head up to the room and close the door.

Sasha looks at Kelly and asked "So what the hell did you two talk about at the sculpture park."

"Nothing, I'll tell you later." Kelly said.

"okay, fine, now what are you doing."

"I am making a dinner plan with Amanda, since your going out with Paige, I figure I would take my new friend and we would meet Amanda" Kelly says as she puts her cell phone to her ear.

Sasha takes Kelly's arm and they walk into the bathroom downstairs. "Okay your going to tell me what the fuck is going on."

'Fine I'll tell you, back in high school Amanda was in love with this woman and when she told her, this women rejected her and made fun of her, so that is the reason she had all of us, and then she also had a crush on me when she was first dating my brother which didn't make it much better, and then come to find out that the women was Amanda, so to make a long story short we are going to confront Amanda tonight and Rebecca is going to give her a piece of her mind."

"that's what you two took almost two hours to talk about."

"yeah, basically. So are you okay with all of this." Kelly asked

'I guess, as long as she doesn't try to do something stupid at our wedding."

"I don't think that will be an issue."

"Good, then have fun tonight, and I won't tell Paige were you are."

Kelly gives Sasha a kiss on the cheeks then on the lips "Thanks and I love you honey"

They both walk out of the bathroom just as Rebecca and Steven come down the stairs. Rebecca gives Kelly a smile as she kisses Steven on the lips. Then she walks over to Kelly and smiles as she walks pass and into the kitchen. Sasha gives Kelly a stern look.

"what, she's doing that for god knows why." Kelly replied

"Right, I trust you honey." Sasha said, then she mumble something in Russian that Kelly could hardly hear.

"What."

"nothing, go and have fun with Amanda and Rebecca" Sasha finished as she lightly slapped Kelly on the ass and then walked away.

Kelly walks into the kitchen and sits across from Rebecca and says 'Okay we'll meet Amanda for dinner at 5:00 , she'll be at CoHo's."

'The one in Issaquah."

"yeah, so we have time before we have to leave." Kelly says

Rebecca nods as she eats the sandwich that she had just finished fixing her self. An hour had past since Kelly made the arrangements to meet with Amanda, Rebecca was upstairs taking a shower. She was barely able to hear Kelly when she told her to hurry up, they are leaving shortly. Rebecca got out of the shower and started to dry off, when she was remembering back in school, how much she loved Amanda, And how much Amanda turned that love into something funny and shameful. Now she was confronting the woman who broke her heart and embarrassed her the rest of the school year. She got dressed and met Kelly down stairs.

'Okay I'm ready." Rebecca walks downstairs in a short plaid schoolgirl type skirt and a tight pink blouse that made her breast bigger then they really were. Mind you her breast are b y no means small in the first place.

"Wow, you look great." Kelly says looking at Rebecca.

Rebecca smiles and replies 'Well do I look fuckable."

"Very, if I might say."

"Thank you." Rebecca says.

"Then lets go." Turns her head back to Sasha and adds 'Enjoy Honey, and I'll see you later."

Kelly and Rebecca leave the house, Rebecca has her am over Kelly's as they walk to the car. Sasha looks at Steven and gives him a shrugged and replied "don't look at me , I have clue the plans that Kelly comes up with sometimes."

"that's great my wife is going and confronting someone that she hasn't seen in years that broke her heart." Steven said sounding a little up set.

"I know, but I do believe that Kelly would never let anything happen to Rebecca." Sasha comforted Steven.

"Thanks that actually helps, coming from you"

"I'll take that as a compliment, I think"

Sasha and Steven headed to the kitchen, and talked a little more, until Sasha had to and meet up with Paige. She suggest that Steven come along and meet Paige. It took a few minutes of convincing but Steven agreed and they left together. Leaving Hannah with her grandchildren, which she never minded she loved the twins to death. They were always spoiled by their grandparents and then by their grandmother since their grandfather died last year. But Hannah had finally gotten over it, it was rough the first few months but since she has moved into Steven and Rebecca's house with his family, she has gotten a new lease on life.   So for now everything is quite wonderful, even when Kelly and Rebecca arrive at the restaurant. Kelly and Rebecca are shown to their seat, the waiter has told then that the other lady as not yet arrived and that he will show her to the table when she does.

"So do you know what your going to say to Amanda when she does show up." Kelly asked.

"no not really, I figure I would say what ever comes to my mind, even though that is a very dangerous thing to do." Kelly said as she took a sip of her glass of water.

Moments later the matre'de walks over and sits Amanda down with Kelly and Rebecca.

Amanda looks at Rebecca, smiles and replies to Rebecca "Well Hello there may I say you look very hot."

Rebecca smiles back and says as she gets up "Thank you" then she sits back down once Amanda sits down.

"Thanks for inviting me out Kelly, and to bring a friend along with you" Amanda says trying to sit close to Rebecca. Rebecca doesn't seem to mind, she hasn't tried moving. Then Amanda turns and looks at Rebecca and adds "So what is it that you do?"

"Well I am a school teacher, but I took some time off to come to Kelly and Sasha's wedding." Rebecca says as she moves her hand closer to Amanda's. While all the time Kelly is watching what Rebecca is doing which is flirting with Amanda? The waitress walks up. And she is a pretty waitress. All three of them stare at her when they give the waitress their order. She nods repeats the order and walks away. Rebecca gets up and excuses her self then walking to the bathroom. A few seconds later with a bit of a surprise is followed by Amanda.

Amanda makes sure that there is no one else in the restroom, she then waits until Rebecca gets out of the stall and walks over to the sink. Amanda walks over to her takes her by the arm and plants a big passionate kiss onto Rebecca's lips.

"God I've wanted to do that since high school."

Rebecca standing there in shock, then after a few seconds more replies. 'wait you knew who I was the whole time."

"Yes, And before you say one word I am truly sorry on how I treated you in school, I had the biggest crush on you too, but my friends would not have been my friends if I told them that I liked girls and one that was in band."

'holy shit, do you know what I have done, and how I treated people because of what you did to me in school." Rebecca shouts.

"I'm sorry, could we start over again."

"I wish I could, but I am married and twins that are five now."

'Ok come on I have dreamed that I would meet you again, and that we could work out the problems."

"And what live happily ever after, well that doesn't exist in the real world, that's what I thought with my husband, and we have been on the verge of divorce a few times." Rebecca says as she does moves close to Amanda and adds. "Well we could be friends and see where that would lead."

"I can deal with that." Amanda said as she gives Rebecca another kiss on the lips.

"Do you kiss all of your friends like that."

"Oh just the ones that I want to get into bed."

Rebecca blushes "okay I can see that this friendship is going to be different."

Amanda nods they leave the bathroom, and as they begin heading to the table Rebecca takes her hand and puts into Amanda's hand, and they finish walking to the table. Kelly is business eating her salad to notice that they were holding hands.

"My god, what the hell were you two doing in there making out."

"No why what did you see."

"Nothing Rebecca, but you two seem to be friendly now, what the hell is up."

Rebecca leans across the table and answers "Well she knew I was and she was mean just because of her friends."

"Oh well I guess that makes it alright then." Kelly said a little louder.

"No, but she apologized and we are going to try to be friends now!"

"well I guess if that is what you want, and if you are fine with it, "

Rebecca nods her head as she begins to eat her salad and drink some of the wine that the waitress brought to the table. They ate almost everything, and really didn't save any room for dessert. They left the restaurant together, Amanda and Rebecca gave each other a goodbye kiss and parted ways for the evening. Kelly and Rebecca got into Kelly's car and they drove home. They were silent all the way until Kelly got to her street.

"So what are you going to tell my brother, because he is going to ask how tonight went?"

"I know and I'll tell him the truth."

Kelly stopped the car in the middle of the road, and looked right into Rebecca's eyes. "you are going to tell Steven that you were flirting and ready to jump the bones of the woman you wanted to get revenge on since high school."

"yeah roughly it, why should I not."

"Okay first he just found out this afternoon that his wife is bisexual and that she doesn't hate gay people."

"what to much info for one day."

"YES, first wait a few days and then ease into him with it, and make up a story, don't tell him you two were making out at the table."

'Hey we're not making out, mind I wouldn't mind it, but we weren't."

Kelly starts the car up again and they pull into the drive a few minutes later. All the light are out, as they get out of the car.

"Okay that's odd, someone should be home." Kelly says as she carefully walks up to the house.

Looking around she doesn't see anything out of the usual, Rebecca gets to the door a few seconds after. Kelly unlocked the door and carefully opened it. The two women walked in, and noticed that Hannah was a sleep on the couch with the twin on each side of her. They walk over to the couch and gently place a blanket over the three of them, and quietly walk to the kitchen.

"I wonder were Steven is." Rebecca asked.

"I don't know unless he went with Sasha to go and meet with Paige." Kelly said as she put some water on for tea. Then she added "would you like some tea."

Looking at her watch "No, I should get to bed, but I would like to thank you for this evening, I had a good time, even if it turned out different from what I planned or even better."

"Your welcome Rebecca" Kelly said as she held out her hand waiting for Rebecca, but instead she leaned in and gave Kelly a kiss ion the cheeks. Then she headed up to the room she was staying in.

About twenty or so minutes later, Kelly lost track of time, from being so tired Sasha and Steven both came in overtly drunk. They were hanging off of each other trying to stay up.

Kelly walks into the living room and walks them into the kitchen and lets then sit down in the chairs.

"what the fuck happened to you two."

'Oh nothing sweetheart." Steven said as Sasha and Steven started laugh uncontrollably.

In a softer voice Kelly tried to quiet those two down "Guys your going to wake the twins"

Then Sasha and Steven put their fingers over their mouths and went "shhhh".

"Okay that's enough, Steven go up stairs, and you go in to the den." Kelly said in her commanding voice.

"Oh look sashy mommies sending us to our rooms." Steven said as they continued to giggle.

Kelly stood in front of then and gave them an evil stare and folded her arms "Now you two do what I said."

Steven staggered upwards and tried to bow, but almost fell over, he eventually made it upstairs and into bed. Kelly helped Sasha into the den and placed her on the couch, with a bucket on the side of her. Then she got into the sleeping bag and fell asleep her self. The next morning Sasha had woken up with such a hang over .

"Oh god, my head, promise one thing honey"

"WHAT'S THAT SASHA" Kelly shouted.

Sasha held her head and barely replied "Please don't do that, and don't let me drink that much ever."

'I'm sorry, and besides I wasn't there, my brother was and he was as drunk as you."

Steven come walking into the den very slowly and whisper "What the hell hit me a meteor."

"NO, it was a bar." Rebecca says in a semi loud voice and then she adds. "Those hangovers serves as a reminder that you shouldn't drink so much."

"Yes honey I know, you told me that upstairs." Steven says quietly.

Sasha turns and puts her head onto Kelly's lap and closes her eyes as she says "I want to die."

'I'm sure you do honey." Kelly says as she pats Sasha's head.

Well after Sasha and Stevens hangover and headache they all went out and walked around the water front of downtown Seattle. They stopped at the Pirates Plunder Shop on the pier and found a few interesting Items that a friend of Sasha and Kelly's. Then they went and checked out the Maritime museum, and after a while Hannah and the twins were getting hungry so they decided to stop at Red Robin. That two a good hour and a half, it was like almost everyone in Seattle had the same Idea. But then after everyone was done the finished their little walk by walking over to the Pikes Place Market, Sasha and Kelly had been their lots of times, but the rest of the family hasn't, so they had a good time especially the twins. They returned back home really late in the evening the twins were fast a sleep in the car, so Steven had to carry them in to the house. As soon as Rebecca got out of the car, her cell started to vibrate. And she looked at the id on it and it was Amanda.

"Hello" Rebecca said as she answered it.

"Hi there cutie, it's Amanda, what are you doing right now." Amanda asked.

"Well nothing, just going into the house, we spent the whole day in Seattle."

"Sounds exciting, do you want to come over, I rented this cool movie"

Sounding a bit excited "What's it called."

"The title is Loving Annabelle, it's really a good movie, I think you'd like it."

"The title sounds good. I'll see if I can sneak out okay."

'Cool, I'll see you."

Before Amanda hangs up she gives Rebecca her address. Then Rebecca walks into the house, and takes Kelly aside and asked what she should do, and then asked to help her sneak out, so she could go and see Amanda.

'I don't know Amanda, do you think you really should." Kelly whispered back to her.

"Oh, please I'll owe you."

"Okay fine, lets go before they come down stairs." Kelly says grabbing her keys and phone from the table by the door.

Sasha comes out of the kitchen and sees a note laying on the coffee it reads, "Be back soon , willc all to tell you, love Kelly."

"That's odd" Sasha says to her self."

Chapter Five

The morning day before the wedding, Hannah has finally convinced Sasha and Kelly to sleep apart from each other until tomorrow after the wedding. So Kelly had rented a hotel room for the few days. And to keep her company, her sister in law came along. Who had ulterior motives to be in a hotel room. They did rent separate room, so Sasha and Steven would not worry, Rebecca was laying on her bed reading a magazine when there was a knock. She gets up fast and quickly walks over to the door.

'Yes, who is it." Rebecca ask

"Room Service" Amanda's voice replied.

Rebecca opens the door and sees Amanda standing there in a long coat. She grabs Amanda's hand and pulls her into the room. And as the door closes the two women begin to kiss each other. Amanda removed her coat revealing just a bra and a pair of panties.

"Oh how much I've missed you the last couple of days." Amanda said as she kissed all around Rebecca's face and neck.

'I've missed you too, I want you right now." Rebecca said.

They move each other to the closer of the two beds in the room. Then Amanda gently laid Rebecca onto her back on the bed. All the time still kissing each other, Rebecca couldn't remove her clothes fast enough, and Amanda helped a little, removing her blouse. Rebecca got her skirt unzipped and threw it across the room hitting the desk. Amanda moved down and started to kiss Rebecca's breast that were not covered by her bra. Then Amanda cupped her hands over Rebecca's breast and moved the bra aside, exposing her perky nipples.

"Oh yes, make love to me." Rebecca said in a passionate whisper.

"Yes ma'am" Amanda said as she moves down Rebecca's stomach kissing her bare skin. She stops when she gets to

Rebecca's panties then she starts kissing Rebecca's panties and moves over her pussy and starts licking it through the panties. Then Amanda takes her fingers and slowly moves them up Rebecca's leg and over her thigh until she gets them to Rebecca's panties and slides them under. She starts to rub the tip of her clit as she continues to kiss and lick the panty area. Rebecca is in a state of ecstasy as she moans with pleasure. Keeping her finger down between Rebecca's legs and letting them explore her pussy, Amanda moves back up and continues kissing her on the lips, adding her tongue into Rebecca's mouth now and then. Saying sexy words as she enters Rebecca's hole with two of her fingers. Rebecca arches are back a slight and moans even louder now.

"I love you" came rolling out of Rebecca's mouth as she was continuing to get fingered by Amanda. Amanda just smiled and then stuck two more fingers inside of her. Thrusting in and out with all but her thumb inside of Rebecca, she started to move them in and out faster and faster. Rebecca began to squirm around, not able to control herself.

She screams out loud "Oh, fuck yes, make me cum."

Amanda continued to kiss her at the same time as she replied "I'm trying baby." Amanda takes her free hand and unsnaps the front latch of Rebecca's bra releasing the rest of her breast. She moves her mouth down and begins to suck on Rebecca's erect nipples. Rebecca moans more and screams that she is about to cum. With out any more warning, Rebecca starts to squirt and then she realises a big orgasm wetting her panties and Amanda's hand. Amanda pulls her fingers out from Rebecca's pussy and then from underneath the panties. Slowly moving them up Rebecca's body, stopping her hands at Rebecca's breast , then she rubbed her wet fingers around Rebecca's nipples then lick her finger the rest of the way clean.

"I love the way you taste." Amanda said as she gave Rebecca another kiss on the lips.

Rebecca catching her breathe replies in a shallow voice "Thank you, I love the way you make me cum."

Then a knock came on the door. Amanda and Rebecca looked at each other Amanda quickly grabbed her clothes and ran into the bathroom. Rebecca got up put a robe on and walked towards the door.

"I'm coming hold on." She said as she gets to the door and opens it up, letting a breathe of relief seeing that it was just Kelly she adds "Oh thank god, its just you."

'Oh, well I'm glad to see you too, and you can have Amanda come out of the bathroom." Kelly says as she walks in and closes the door.

Amanda walks out of the bathroom, still just in her bra and panties. 'How did you know I was here.'

"Um you two, I think the whole hotel knows that you two are here." Kelly replied.

Rebecca starts to blush and moves closer to Amanda. Then Kelly adds "Okay your suppose to be making sure that I don't have sex, and I'm sure that your not suppose to have sex either, SINCE YOUR MARRIED."

"I know , but I wanted to live out my fantasy, and sleep with the woman I fell in love with back in high school."

" I know that, but you have my brother and the twins back at my house, what about them." Kelly asks as she looks at both Amanda and Rebecca.

"I love your brother, but I just want this right now, your brother and I haven't really had sex for a long time, and I will never give up my children, they are the world."

"Then, just tell Steven that you are in love with Amanda and get it over and done with, I'm sure my brother can take it, he's lived with a lesbian for a long time, so I think he'll be fine with it." Kelly said then she turned around and left the room.

Rebecca looked at Amanda and the said. "What should I do, I don't want to loose you a second time."

"You won't I'll be there for you no matter what" Amanda said as she gave Rebecca a kiss.

Rebecca smiles and gives Amanda a hug "thanks," Rebecca walks over to the dresser and pulls out a bra, then she gets a skirt and blouse from the closet and walks in to bathroom.

"Becky, did you forget something."

Rebecca looks around "Oh yes thanks." She walks back to the dresser and grabs a pair of nylons and a garter belt then back to the bathroom.

"What about your panties."

'What about them" she smiles and closes the bathroom door.

Amanda looks at the pair of panties that she pulled from the drawer, then smiled as she put them back and walked towards the bathroom, turning the knob and slowly opening the door. Thinking to herself "Good she didn't lock the door." Amanda walks in hearing the shower run, and seeing Rebecca's nude silhouette pressed up against the door. She removes her bra and panties, then she slides the door open, staring at Rebecca's wet and soapy body, she climbs in takes the bar of soap from Rebecca and starts to soap herself.

"Hey I'm taking a shower here." Rebecca said in a soft non serious tone.

"I know I need one too." Amanda replied back. Then she takes the soap and starts to rub it across and over Rebecca's breast.

"No, it's my turn then to make love to you." Rebecca said as she takes the soap from Amanda's hand and starts to soap up Amanda's breast. Then rinsing them off she moved her mouth over to Amanda's nipples and began to suck on them. Just as Rebecca was about to go down on Amanda there was a knock on the door again. Then the door slowly opened and Kelly stuck her head in and heard the shower running and said "Don't you two ever give up, god. Hurry up we have an appointment with the beauty salon in twenty minutes."

Amanda stuck her head out and replied as she was catching her breathe "We'll be there in a minute."

"Well just hurry up." Kelly closed the door again. Amanda closes the shower door and gives Rebecca a look.

"What, she paid for the room, so she got a spare key."

"Well I guess that's fine." Amanda says as they go back to kissing. Then Rebecca drops the soap, and grabs onto Amanda, their breast pressing against each other.

"I don't want this to end." Rebecca says.

Amanda running her hand through Rebecca's wet long hair as she replies "I don't either, but if we don't Kelly will come back in here and drag our asses out clothed or not."

"I know, so we should get dressed and make Kelly happy, since her wedding day is tomorrow." Rebecca finished as she turned off the water, and started to get out of the shower, then she was pulled back in by Amanda.

"we have time" Amanda said as she moved her hands up and down Rebecca's side.

"we do, but lets make Kelly happy just this once." Rebecca said as she took Amanda's hands into her own and got out of the shower tugging Amanda along with her.

"I guess we could." Amanda says then she adds, "I have a serious question"

"Shoot, what is it" Rebecca says as she starts to get dressed.

"Do you ever wonder what you life would be like now, if I didn't do what my friends in high school wanted."

"Back in the day, but I had gotten over that I just live for the now, I never worry about what tomorrow will bring, or how my life would have been if I did something didn't, why."

'Oh, no reason, but I have recently, the other night, I was a wake thinking about you and wondering if I took that step back in school would we still be together."

"I'm sure," Rebecca says as she puts her blouse on. Then adds " I'm still with my husband after a long time, and you I have loved before him."

"You said you loved me, with out having sex."

"yes I did and I still love you now"

Amanda gets close to Rebecca and gives her a very passionate kiss.

'I love you too, Rebecca I want to spend my life with you. "

Rebecca stood there speechless for a few seconds. 'I don't what to say, now I will have to talk with Steve, and figure something out."

"I suggest that you do it after Kelly and Sasha's wedding."

"your right." Rebecca gave Amanda a hug, and then another knock came across the door. Amanda finished getting dressed and Rebecca walked over to the door and opened it. Kelly was standing there looking a little mad.

"Are you two ready yet." Kelly said in an aggressive sounding voice.

"Yes, Amanda just has to put her heels on and we'll be ready , god are you pushy today." Rebecca said.

"well yeah, my big day is tomorrow, so we don't have a lot of time to do everything. And I'll be meeting up with Lisa later so we can go over the stuff we need to do. "

"Okay I'm ready lets go." Amanda says as she walks up next to the girls, and lightly pinches Rebecca's ass. Rebecca jumps a little and looks at Amanda with a small smile. Then all three leave the room heading to the elevator. Once they get to the first floor of the hotel, Kelly points to the direction of the hotels beauty salon. They walk in that direction.

"So we're not meeting up with Lisa here." Rebecca asked.

"No, she's getting her hair down at her ex's salon."

"Boy she's daring," Amanda said

"They are on good terms, they we're always better friends, then they we're lovers."

"well that works out then doesn't it."

"Yes." Kelly says as they walk into the salon. A tall Scandinavian blonde woman walks up to Kelly and the other girls then ask if she could help them. Kelly told her, what her last name is and that she had an appointment for two others also. The woman nodded and walked each one of them to separate chairs and said that their hair dresser will be with then shortly. They were in the salon for about two hours. They all had their hair, nails done, the salon even did bikini waxes on all of them. Kelly was the first one done, as Kelly was waiting for the other two she felt a hand on her shoulder, quickly turning around she saw the love of her life Sasha. She stands up and they embrace in a kiss as Kelly says "Oh my god you can't believe how lonely I've been for the last four days. "

"I can, I had trouble sleeping, those night too."

Kelly looks around "So how did you sneak away from my mother."

"I just told her I was going to the gym so can fit into my wedding gown a little better."

"And she bought that."

"Yes, lets go to your room, I want you so badly that I have pains."

Kelly rubs Sasha's arms and replies. "I wish I could but, some how my mother would find out, and beside I have to be the look out for Steve, since Rebecca is having an affair with Amanda."

Sasha has a surprise look on her face "Still, I figured Amanda would have dumped her by now."

"No, I think they could be soulmates or something, they act like they have been together since their high school days."

"Okay that's just plain creepy."

"tell me about it, you know what, lets go up to my room, and then you wouldn't be lying to my mother."

"I like that kind of exercise."

Kelly walks back into the salon and tells the receptionist to tell her two friends that she needed to go do something and that they can do what they want with in reason. The receptionist nodded and Kelly left, grabbing onto Sasha's hand then they took the elevator up to Kelly's room. By the time they got there they were all over each other.

'Oh god, how I missed your hands running over my body, Rip my clothes off and do what ever you want with me." Kelly said as she opened the hotel room door and nearly fell into the room."

Sasha barely got into the room, when her jogging pants and sports bra was already off. Helping with removing Kelly's clothes they inched their way to the bed. Sasha was all over Kelly kissing her neck, then moving down to her breast and then Sasha sucks on Kelly's nipples. Kelly moans as she falls onto the bed, with Sasha falling on top of her. Sasha continues moving down Kelly's body kissing each inch of it. She them moves back up and kisses Kelly on the lips again.

"I love you." Kelly said as she moved her hand down Sasha's back. Every once in a while digging her manicured nails into Sasha's back. Sasha releases a small scream.

"Oh sorry" Kelly whispers

"No, that felt good, it was a pleasurable scream, my love" Sasha replied with a bit of her Russian ascent coming through. Then they both roll over and Sasha ends up on her back.

"No it's my turn to pleasure you. " Kelly said as she tweaks and pulls on Sasha's nipple rings.

"Da, Da ebat" Sasha moaned

Kelly got even more excited when she heard Sasha speak Russian, It made her that much hornier and wanting to fuck her lover that much more. She couldn't wait, she moved down as quickly as she could to Sasha's cleaned shaven pussy took her tongue and lightly went over Sasha's clit and lips licking up some of her moisture. Sasha let out another moan in Russian so Kelly did it again. Then with no warning Kelly stops and gets up. Sasha catches her breathe.

"Kel what you stopped."

"Yes, I was saving this for our honeymoon , but think of it as a pre-wedding gift from me." Kelly says as she goes over to her back , pulls out a harness with a long rubbery dildo attached to it. Kelly smiles as she strapped it on.

"Now, I want to fuck you, like you've never been fucked."

Sasha gives out a little smile and moves her legs apart farther, Kelly rubs the dildo with vaginal lube then walks back over to Sasha lying on the bed. Kelly slowly moves between Sasha's legs and with little teasing she inserts the dildo right into Sasha's pussy. Sasha moves back a little and then arches her back as she releases a pleasurable moan. Kelly moved in and out in a steady motion, then she slowly sped up as she grabbed onto Sasha's thighs. Sasha's moaning got more erratic as Kelly continue to up the speed of her thrusting. Then Sasha arched her back more and cried out in Russian.

"ebat ma-yo manda " (fuck my pussy)

Those were the few words Kelly actually knew in Russian, because Sasha would usually say that right before she would cum. So Kelly went faster and deeper, and as she did she too was ready to cum. Hoping that they would come together, so it would be a special one last moment before they were to be married. They please each other for the next hour and half, Kelly is extremely tired afterwards. She lays down on Sasha's lap,

"Honey, I should go now, our wedding is tomorrow, and I'm sure your mother will come looking for me." Sasha said in her sweet Russian accented voice.

Kelly looked up and quietly replied. "I know she will my mother has been persistent on keeping us from having sex until our wedding night for the last month."

Sasha helps Kelly up off of her lap, and then she slowly gets up and puts her jogging pants back on followed by her sports bra. Giving Kelly the last kiss on the lips until they are at the altar, Sasha says as she walks towards the door. "I love you." Kelly looked at her and said the same. Sasha walks out the door, and looks around the hallway. The door closes and she makes her way to the elevator, the door opens, Amanda and Rebecca are inside the elevator. Amanda smiles as Rebecca giggles.

"Okay you two not a word." Sasha says as she walks into the elevator.

"I won't say a word, I promise" Amanda says with a little giggle then.

"Yeah, I hope you left Kelly with some energy, she meeting Lisa later." Rebecca said as she joined Amanda outside of the elevator.

"She will never forget this night" Sasha says as the elevator doors close.

Amanda and Rebecca looks at each other and then Amanda says "I wonder what she means by that.

"I don't know, but we need to get Kelly anyway so we could ask her." Rebecca responded. Amanda nodded and so they headed to Kelly's hotel room. By the time they got there Kelly had just gotten enough energy to get up, she answered the door still in the nude.

"oh great Kelly, have you forgotten about meeting Lisa in ten minutes."

"Oh fuck, I did, I'll be right out let me throw something on." Kelly says as she pulls the two girls in to the room and closes the door. And finds a bra and a pair of panties, after putting then on she slips into a pair of jeans and a loose t-shirt.

"Okay I'm ready top go and meet with lisa."

Amanda and Rebecca both look at each other and shrug their shoulders. "Okay then lets go have some fun at your bachalorette party."

"Yeah, even though I remember saying that I didn't want one." Kelly said in a monotone voice.

"oh come when has that ever stopped any of us." Amanda said.

The three of them leave the room arm in arm and they begin skipping down they hall towards the elevator. Then out of nowhere Amanda starts whistling the "The Wizard of Oz tune" then Rebecca joins in by say 'We're off to see the wizard, the wonderful wizard of oz."

Kelly looks at both of them and makes a comment "Okay you two smart asses, you can knock it off."

They get to the elevator and take it down to the lobby where the hotel staff has a car waiting for them to take them to Lisa's secret party place. They get into the car and leave, after about ten minutes the car arrives at the location. The driver gets out and opens the door for them, Amanda and Rebecca nod and then smile, because they both know the driver was watching and enjoying them both making out with each other. Kelly gets out and apologizes for the both of them and slips him a fifty dollar tip.

"Thank you man, and I kind of enjoyed it, I usually only take stiff suits and corporate people that have no sense of humour or emotions."

Kelly then walks away as the driver closes the door and then he gets back into the car and pulls away and parks with the other cars. Kelly looks around and is amazed that Lisa has gathered this many people for a party, and wondering how much all this has cost the renting of the warehouse and everything. The doors open and Lisa is standing there in lingerie. Kelly walks in first and sees that most everyone is in some kind of lingerie.

"No one said that we had to come in our lingerie." Amanda said

"Well you girls are wearing bras and panties right." Lisa replied

Amanda and Kelly nodded, and then they looked at Rebecca who smiled and then replied back "well not exactly, I'm going commando under my dress."

Amanda walks closely to Rebecca with a wide smile and says in a flirty tone "Oh really, maybe we should leave."

"Oh no, you two aren't leaving, if I have to stay so are you." Kelly says as she walks in between them both. Lisa follows Kelly and takes her arm. They all join the party. There are some girls making out in the far corner of the warehouse. But most everyone has their attention on Lisa and Kelly. Lisa has Kelly sit in a chair that is in the centre of the room and Lisa puts on a microphone headset and then stands behind her.

"Okay ladies the guest of honour has arrived, so now the party can really begin." Lisa says, then music starts to play, and lights all zoom to the small stage and two girls start doing a strip dance show. Kelly's chair slowly moves close to the stage.

The girls dancing come closer to Kelly and start too provocatively dance around Kelly and the chair. One starts to strip and she throws her clothes to other women who are standing around. Then the dancer pushes Kelly's legs together and starts to give her a lap dance, while all the time all the party guess are hooting and hollering at the two dancer. Kelly looks around and pretends to be embarrassed but she's not really. Kelly is enjoying it, surprise that Lisa was able to find two good looking non-whore looking strippers for her party. The dancer finished taking the rest of her clothes off, and ran her panties across Kelly's body and left them on her lap and the started to grind her bare ass on Kelly's lap doing the reversed cowgirl. Then she stops and goes back to the pole, after a while the girls stop dancing and Kelly is able to get up from the chair. Joss Stone's Tell Me 'Bout it starts to play through the speakers.

'Oh I love this song." Rebecca said and she starts to dance to the music, she even grabs Amanda to start dancing with her.

Paige walks up to Kelly and gives her a hug.

"Paige" Kelly says sounding a bit surprised.

"Oh don't worry, I'm over her let someone else deal with her psychoness." Paige said

"oh good, I was hoping there wouldn't be any fighting anymore, hey I heard that you were in England helping Scotland Yard."

"Yeah, I needed to help a few friends, So I'll tell you about it later."

"Sounds good. I'm glad you're here."

"I wouldn't miss two of my best friends finally getting married." Paige said with a smile.

Paige and Kelly get on the dance floor and start dancing. Amanda glances over and is amazed that Paige showed up "oh wow she's here."

"Who honey." Rebecca said.

Amanda pointed to Paige and replied "See that woman dancing with Kelly, that is Paige Sinclair my ex."

Rebecca pulls Amanda closer to her and says "Please don't start anything." .

Amanda gives Rebecca a kiss on the lips. "Don't worry I'm not going to do anything, I promise."

Rebecca smiles "Thank you." Rebecca and Amanda continue to dance as everyone else on at the party. It seems to going smoothly Lisa thinks to her self, hopefully Jo pulled one good party off for Sasha.

At Sasha and Kelly's house, there is music coming from indoors, a couple of police cars are parked in the driveway. Inside the house Sasha, Jo and other girls are having fun, The two police cars belong to two of Jo's ex-flings that she invited, for the simple reason, if cop cars are already there, then the neighbours will not likely call for more no matter how noisy it gets. Jo has made a great party for Sasha.

But it is nothing like that of Kelly's, then again different friends and different taste.

Sasha walks over to Jo. "Thanks for the party , its great, how about a game of pool."

Jo looks around and sees that all the women and the few guys that are their friends enjoys sports on the big screen TV and others just standing around talking. "Sure, I enjoy our game of pool."

Sasha and Jo head to the den where the pool table is, they walked in just as two women were just finishing their set. The two women walked over to Sasha and Jo and asked if they wanted to join them in a game. Jo and Sasha nodded. So all four women started to play, They played a lot of games.

The parties are over and now everyone at both locations have finally fallen asleep. When morning comes no one wants to move or even get up. Jo looks at the clock and sees that they still have a t least five hours before they have to get Sasha to the church. So she figured the she would co and check on her. Jo got up and looked around for Sasha and to her surprise she found her in bed in the arms of some women that one of their mutual friends brought to the party. Jo walks over to the bed and wakes Sasha up .

"Sasha, wake up."

Sasha moves a little and throws her arm around the woman next to her, and slowly opens her eyes. Looking around she notices that she is in bed with someone that is not Kelly. Quickly jumping out of the bed .

"Ok fuck, did I do something last night, Jo I can't remember."

"I don't think so." Jo replied back looking around the room at other sleeping women.

"Good, I can't believe I almost did something like that especially on the night before my wedding."

"I would have hated to tell Kelly on our wedding day that I did something stupid." Sasha said in a worried voice.

"But you don't so there is nothing to worry about."

"Yeah your right, let me go and take a shower then, we can go and have some breakfast."

"sounds good, I'll tell Darlene to help clean up, and that I'll be back in a little while. "

Sasha nods her head and then grabs some clothes and heads towards the bathroom. Jo looks around the room, and then leaves going back downstairs, and finds Darlene just waking up. She walks over to her and tells Darlene that she is taking Sasha out for breakfast and that she needs to get the house cleaned up . Darlene agrees. So after Sasha had taken a quick shower and gotten dressed, Jo and her had left for a Shari's or Denny's somewhere they could sit down, talk and eat something that will settle the butterflies in Sasha's stomach. They arrived at a Shari's and they waited to be seated, once they had been the waitress came by and poured them some coffee and tea, and then took their order.

"I am glad we became friends and that April found some one, besides trying to lust after my girlfriend." Sasha said starting the conversation.

"Me too who would have guessed that April would have suggested, that I come over and help install your new bathroom downstairs?"

"I'm glad I actually listen to her, because I don't know who I would have picked for the head best women."

"It's a shame that April and Oksana are on a vacation, April is going to be mad that she missed Kelly and your wedding."

"Well they did send a card and a gift, saying that they were sorry, and that Oksana's mother is doing better now, and she wishes that she was able to still be the brides maid for Kelly."

"That's good, all she sent her oldest friend was a post card and that she love living in the Czech Republic for now."

"That's good, and that another friend of Kelly's volunteered to be her bridesmaid".

"So if I might ask , how long have Kelly and Lisa known each other."

"Oh god all their life, matter of fact they first told each other that they liked girls and even dated, but decided that they were better off as friends. "

"oh wow, I don't know if I could date someone and then decide to be friends if it didn't work out."

"Me neither, but that's Kelly for you always trying to make and keep as many friends as she could gather. "

" She seems like that kind of person, I think you two are going to be great for each other, and I hope by the goddess that your marriage last. Which reminds me,"

"Whats that Jo."

"Oh your remember meeting my friend Cory and Natalie."

"Yeah, I thought that they were perfect for each other, why."

'Oh, they're getting a divorce."

Sasha looks surprised,"what how, they seemed that that they loved each other."

'oh they did, but it seems that Natalie, got up one morning and started to pack her bags, and was ready to leave, when she turned to Cory and said that she is straight, and she could live this way anymore. So she left and now with her boy friend she is fighting for custody of their two children."

"Oh god, I hate to be that lawyer, taking that mess on, and I'm sure that it will not be an easy divorce."

"Me too Cory even tried to get Abernathy to talk to Natalie to see if she would change her mind."

"That there is an unique person a man that hangs out with lesbians and helps then stay together. No man would normally do that, most men have that two girl fantasy and want to be in it, but not him his fantasy is to keep lesbian couples together by helping with their problems. So I'm assuming that he failed.

"Oh, big time and now he has a small church group from Natalies boyfriends family breathing down his neck."

"poor guy, one of the few men I really do like, and I would have no trouble having him around."

"I know what you mean."

"Now he has to deal with them."

"I wouldn't worry about it, he's good, besides I hope Cory wins the case, she has been a good friend for a long time."

Sasha and Jo finish their breakfast, Jo picked up the tab and then they left. Jo suggest that they go and do a few things before heading back to the house. Sasha agreed, so they decided to head to the market in Seattle, since Sasha and Kelly will not see it for a couple of weeks while they are on their Honeymoon. Walking around the market , which isn't to busy this morning as it is just opening. Then Sasha's cell ring, playing a Brandi Carlile song. She answers it and it is Kelly's mother, telling her that she should be returning home soon, because she has a gift for her. Sasha agreed and said that she will return home in about thirty minutes. Then she tells Jo and they finish what they were doing and headed back to Sasha's house on Capital hill.

"Oh before I forget Sasha here, I thought you and Kelly would like to use this." Jo hands Sasha an envelope.

Sasha takes it and opens it up " Oh thanks this is cool, but how did you get these we don't live in California." Sasha asked as she hold two passes for Skysports and Spa.

"An Ex of mine is a client and she loves the place, so I asked her to see if Mrs. Warner would like to extend an invitation to a couple of people in Washington."

"Oh I can't wait to tell Kelly, she's a big fan of the show workout and Jackie Warner." Sasha finishes as she gives Jo a hug.

They get back to Sasha's house, and Darlene has done a superb job on getting the house cleaned up. If she didn't know better, Sasha would never have guessed that there was a party here last night. She gives Darlene a hug and thanks her for cleaning the house. Darlene explains to her that it was nothing, her and her sisters did it all the time when they were in high school, they always had to make sure the house was clean and there was no sign of any kind of party, so she had gotten good at it. Sasha tells the girls that she is going up stairs to take a long hot shower, and to get ready for her wedding day. Jo and Darlene go and get her clothing ready that Sasha wants to wear under her dress, and then they pulled out the dress.

Darlene holds up the dress and looks at Jo. "So honey, are we ever going to get married."

Jo looks at Darlene walks over to her and replies. "Sure at some point in time, but right now this is Sasha and Kelly's time."

Kelly is just getting up and having a little breakfast with her friends and brides maids. Lisa gives Kelly a hug, and then ask her to tell how Sasha proposed to her and how she said yes. Kelly agreed, and then everyone come and sits around Kelly.

'So where should I start, Oh yes I was starting the first day of my vacation and Sasha said she had something planned for us that whole week. So I was anxious to see what it was, I raced home io think I broke a few speed laws that day, but I digress. Back to the story. I had gotten home and Sasha was laying on the couch in this sexy lingerie from Victoria Secrets. That's a whole different story. After I came home, she had dinner waiting for me, Sasha went all out she made lobster with all the trimmings and bought an expensive bottle of wine. We sat down and had a wonderful dinner."

"And a wonderful few too, I'm assuming." Lisa interrupted. Then Paige smacked Lisa on her shoulder as Paige said. "Shush, we want to hear the story."

Kelly continues "Thank you, okay so after dinner she got dressed and showed me tickets to the ballet, it was a good show. I really enjoyed that, then before we got home she drove to the Edmonds beach and walked around for a while, and as we walked she stopped by the water pulled me to close to her and said I love you, and I want to spend my life with you, and then she pulled out a small box and opened it, then she said would you marry me, you are my soul mate. And of course I said yes.

"Oh that's so romantic" Amanda said as she was hugging Rebecca from the back.

All the others round the table agreed and then one by one started to give Kelly a hug. Kelly gets up and they head back to the hotel to prepare for her to get to the wedding on in time.

Chapter Six

The hour has arrived, the guest are arriving at the church. Kelly's brother is helping people to their seats. Hannah is making sure the final touches are perfect. Rebecca and Amanda are helping Kelly with her dress.

"Okay sis you look very beautiful." Rebecca says as she walks around Kelly looking up and down the dress.

'Thank you, I hope Sasha likes it, and that I am going commando too."

"Oh, hell Kel, that will just make the pre honeymoon even that much better, especially when you two throw the garter." Amanda said with a smile.

Kelly looks at Amanda with a look and replies. "Yeah well I want you on your feet and not bending over, got it."

Amanda give Kelly and innocent who me look. "Yeah I got it, you take all the fun out of it."

Then at the moment Rebecca gives Amanda a look and says. "what mines not good enough."

Kelly smiles " God Amanda your in trouble now."

Amanda walks over to Rebecca and rubs her arm "No honey, I love yours, I was just teasing Kelly."

Amanda and Rebecca share a small kiss as Rebecca goes back to adjusting Kelly's dress. "Okay I think we're ready. " Rebecca says.

Amanda leaves the room and heads towards the church area. She walks up to the priest and tells him that everyone is ready. The priest nods to the organ player and she starts to play the old fashion wedding march. Amanda goes and takes her seat. Kelly hears the music playing and nudges to Rebecca and Lisa to go. Rebecca opens the door and they begin to walk out followed by Kelly in her white wedding dress with a long silk veil flowing in the breeze. They hit the hallway once they get into the service area everyone turns and looks at Kelly as she walks in . Sasha ia already standing by the Priest and Jo is to her side. Kelly gave a smile as she made up to the altar and stood next to Sasha. They smiled at each other and then faced the priest. The priest nodded to the two girls and then began to speak.

"We are here today to celebrate the joining of two people who are in love. This is a happy time for them because they have come here to share their love for each other with their family and friends. "Now I would like you two to face each other and Sasha would you repeat after me."

"I Sasha Copulov do take Kelly Walberg to be my wife in love and troubles that are now and in the future. I will protect her and guide her in life as we are a couple."

Sasha repeats the words, and give Kelly another smile. Then the priest looks at Kelly, and ask her to repeat after him, and he says the same thing that he had Sasha to repeat. Then she repeats the words. After that the priest looks at both of them then at the people in the audience, and says that the women also want to add their own vows. He has Sasha go first.

"Kelly we have been for five years, and I could never imagine my life with out you, and wouldn't want to try. I love what we have and I love you."

The priest looks at Kelly and says that she can say her personal vows. "Sasha I to would never want to know what life is like without you. I cherish our love that we have together, and will do anything to make it last. I am glad to be in your life and for you to call me your wife. "

The priest gets a little closer and says. "Not I would by the power invested in me by all these who have come here today pronounce you wife and wife. The priest adds looking at Sasha "You may now kiss your wife." Sasha and Kelly share a long passionate kiss in front of everyone. Then once they are finished the priest takes their hands and says.. "I would like to introduce to you the happy couple Sasha and Kelly Copulov,

The Reception is being held at the west end of the building here, enjoy."

The music starts to play again and this time everyone stands as Kelly and Sasha walk down the aisle holding hands. They leave the area and head back to Kelly's room. Everyone else begins to head to the reception area. Moments later Kelly and Sasha enter the reception still in their wedding dresses. People start to walk up to them and give them hugs, kisses on the cheeks and hand shakes congratulating them on their wedding and how beautiful they look in their dresses and how romantic the wedding seemed with them having their own vows. Then one of the few men there walks up.

"That was very beautiful girls, I don't think I could have planned it better myself." Abernathy said he was a well groomed man that was always trying to keep everyone happy, no matter what the cost to his own life.

Kelly replied back. "Thanks ab, I am so glad you got back from New York in time for the wedding."

"I would never have missed this wedding for the world Kel, you two are made for each other, but I sad that I missed your bachalorette party last night, I heard that it was a good show."

Kelly blushes a little "Oh, don't worry I'm sure some one videoed it for you to add to your collection."

"Oh thanks"

"So how is the big divorce session going with Cory and Natalie."

'Oh, just peachy. And I thought when Paige and Amanda broke up that was messy, that was like a day at the park, compared to Cory and Natalie, what a nightmare, but lets not get in to that now." Abernathy said as he gave Kelly and then Sasha a hug, and mingled with the rest of the party. The Reception went off wonderful, close to the end Kelly sat in a chair lifted her leg up a little showing some leg and Sasha came over and slowly removed Kelly's garter from her leg. Then Kelly stood up , Sasha handed back to her and she begin to twirl it around her finger and then threw it into the crowd, and it landed right onto Abernathy's hand who was sitting down at a table. The both Sasha and Kelly threw the bouquet of flowers and funny thing is that Rebecca and Amanda both caught them. Everyone looks at Amanda and then they smiled. Rebecca started to blush and then Steven walked up and asked her why she was standing anyway. So she told him that they needed to talk later, and not to worry, it wasn't anything bad. After the reception everyone walked Kelly and Sasha out to the waiting limo, where they all gave them more hugs and kisses. Telling them to have a great time on their honeymoon, Kelly began to cry a little saying that she was going to miss them. Sasha reconfide that they are going to be gone for two weeks and all their friends will be here when they get back , with that Kelly felt better , but she still cried as she got into the limo and they left for they airport.

Epilogue

Well it's been about a year since Sasha and Kelly have been back from their honeymoon. They have just celebrated their first anniversary. Those two couldn't be more in love, Now they plan on having a family, Sasha is the one who actually wants to give birth, so they plan on doing a lot to prepare for the major life changing decision. And I am sure they will be happy for a long time to come.

On other notes Rebecca talked to Steven the day after the wedding, she told him that she was in love with Amanda and that she wanted a divorce. Steven gave her one, and the good thing was that even though it could have been an ugly one, Steven and Rebecca agreed on everything, and they have become better friends for it. Surprising to everyone even Paige Amanda is still with her and they seem to doing great. Everyone thinks Amanda has finally found her soulmate. April and Oksana have announce that they are getting married and have invited everyone to come to the

Czech Republic for the wedding. April sold her house and she moved in with Oksana about a month after getting back, but now they more or less live in the Czech State.

It seems that life goes on for everyone good or bad. Paige has gone through a couple of relationship now, but those are completely different stories. Which you will be able to read about as time goes on. Everyone has their ups and downs, so don't let life keep you from what you want go after it. Enjoy and see you all at a later date….

15115444R00107

Made in the USA
Lexington, KY
08 May 2012